I0670902

THE

DEVIL'S

JUSTICE

BY

CHAD CULL

Copyright 2007 Franklin D. Lincoln
All rights Reserved

ISBN 978-0-6151-5486-2

Printed in United States of America

Without limiting the rights under copyright above,
no part of this publication may be reproduced, stored in or
introduced into a retrieval system or transmitted, in any
form or means(electronic, mechanical, photocopying, or
otherwise), without the prior permission of the copyright
owner.

AUTHOR'S NOTE:This is a work of fiction.
Names, characters, places, and incidents either are the
product of the author's imagination or are used fictitiously,
and any resemblance to actual persons, living or dead,
business establishments, or locales is entirely coincidental.

VENGEANCE!

The town marshal stepped up beside Carlin. His gun was still in his hand.

"He fired first, Marshal," Jace said, still watching Egstrom's family. "You saw it."

"Yes, I saw it," the Marshal said with a sigh. His voice was gravelly. "There's nothing I can hold you for, so best you mount up and ride out of town before I can think of something."

Carlin eyed him levelly. "No problem. I got what I came for." He started to turn and walk away.

"And what did you come for?" Asa asked. "Vengeance?"

Jace halted and turned. "No, Marshal," he said flatly. "I came for justice."

"Justice?" Asa said, nodding toward the Egstrom's. "I've heard about you and your so called justice. Call it what you want, but I call it vengeance. And vengeance is the devil's justice. Remember that. And I hope you're satisfied."

Carlin looked him straight in the eye. "I'm satisfied," he said. Then he turned and walked away.

For

Lauren (Abie) Lincoln

The big brother that set the

example for us all.

THE DEVIL'S JUSTICE

Chapter One

The gambler's placid face relaxed and a hint of sparkle appeared in his dark eyes for the first time since the game began three hours ago. It was a lean dark face and crows feet began to crinkle on the sides of his slitted eyes. "Call and raise you another hundred." He tossed a sheaf of bills into the center of the table. The dim light of the overhead lamp shed a cone of orangey glow on the disheveled pot of bills and coins littering the center of the battle scarred wooden table. Wisps of smoke danced in the cone of light.

Three other men sat around the table. The two on each side of the gambler had already tossed in their hands and looked on dejectedly with curious expectations. Only low murmurs of the drinkers at the bar and other tables could be heard in the background.

The young man directly across from the gambler looked up from under dark brooding eyes, his angular jaw, covered with black stubble, set firm and his thin lips pursed with frustration.

THE DEVIL'S JUSTICE

His drooping eyelids lowered to the empty space on the table in front of him where his pile had once been. Dang the luck! He cursed to himself. Finally, a winning hand and he was out of cash. Once again he checked the cards in his hand and grimaced.

"Well?" The gambler prodded, a hint of taunting victory in his deep voice.

Gar Plummer's head jerked upward, eyes flashing with anger beneath the shock of dirty black hair that protruded from beneath his battered hat and splayed out across his low forehead. "Don't rush me," he snarled.

"Take your time, boy," the gambler chided. "When you're ready, just tell me what you're going to do."

"He's cashin' in." A sharp, pitched voice with a Texas drawl, boomed behind Plummer.

The men at the table looked up as Plummer twisted around in his chair and saw the man standing behind him. Gar glanced casually at the man and determining that he did not know him, dismissed the man as a kibitzer and turned immediately back to his cards and the game at hand. He glared at the gambler.

"I said, you're cashin' in, Gar." The voice repeated. There was a hard edge and an icy coldness in the words. The sound of determination and the threat of deadly purpose echoed across the dark barroom. Complete silence took over as the patrons put down their drinks and cringed away, waiting and watching what was shaping up as trouble.

THE DEVIL'S JUSTICE

"Go away, Kid," Gar said with irritation as he glanced once more at the man behind him, and once again turned back to the game.

The man stepped forward behind Plummer, reached over his shoulder and snatched the cards from his hand and tossed them face up in the middle of the table. Aces and Queens.

Enraged, Plummer twisted in his chair and lurching to his feet, his right hand stretching toward the pistol butt protruding from its well worn holster, and froze in mid motion as he stared into the cold black eyes of the man before him. They were brooding eyes. Dangerous, menacing eyes.

"Don't you recognize me, Gar?" The man said though clenched teeth. His jaw set hard. "Take a good look," he demanded, practically growling between his teeth.

The man was not a large man. He stood just over five and a half feet tall, but his shoulders were broad and his body was hard with muscle. At first glance, the man would have been taken as a kid, with his round, ruddy face and apple cheeks. But, looking closer, Gar could see that this man was no kid. This was a man in his mid thirties and he had a seasoned air of confidence. A pistol rode high on his right hip in a well oiled brown holster and his fingers lingered outstretched above the walnut handle.

"Maybe you remember me better from behind and face down in the mud, with rain pelting me and washing away the blood from the hole in my back that you put there."

THE DEVIL'S JUSTICE

Plummer sucked in a lung full of air. He gasped, icy shards creeping up and down his spine and hackles bristling along the back of his swarthy neck. "Carlin?" It was almost a whisper.

Jace Carlin nodded, his grim expression remaining fixed. In his eyes were the memories of that dark rainy night a year and a half ago. The flames of his burning house reflecting in his pupils. The screams of his wife and son screeching in his ears as the raging fire engulfed them. The memory of his brother lying dead beside him. Thunder and lightning crashing and flashing, briefly revealing the cruel, laughing faces of the five men that had attacked them by surprise that fateful night.

"That's right," Carlin said.

Plummer's body began to shake. Suddenly, it all came back to him. "I..I thought you were....."

"Dead?" Carlin finished for him. "I guess I am," he said levelly. "Now you're going to join me." His fingers crept closer to his pistol butt.

Plummer moved quickly, twisting away from the chair and hurling it toward Jace Carlin as he clawed for his own sixshooter.

Carlin dodged away as the chair crashed into his left shoulder and bounced off. He half fell unsteadily to his right, his right shoulder drooping as his fingers snagged the pistol handle and dragged the weapon from its sheath. Searing hot pain burned across the side of his neck as Plummer's gun belched flame and smoke; blood oozing in a stream inside his collar.

THE DEVIL'S JUSTICE

Carlin's own weapon had cleared leather as he fell sideways thumbing the hammer and squeezing the trigger, twice in succession, before his shoulder struck the planking beneath him. Gar Plummer loomed above him, blood covering his entire chest and swaying side to side on rubbery legs and pointing his pistol at Carlin's head, earing the hammer back once more. Carlin raised his pistol and fired again. The impact of the slug drove Plummer backward against the wall, his arms splayed upward and his eyes empty of light. He was already dead as his body slid down the blood streaked wall. Carlin had risen to one knee and fired again at the lifeless body. He squeezed off two more rounds before Plummer landed in a heap on the floor.

Carlin stared blankly at his handiwork. Bile rose in his throat and he suddenly felt sick. His outstretched arm shook violently and he almost dropped his weapon. His jaw began to quiver and he fought back to keep from crying. He had never killed anyone before and he knew this wouldn't be the last for out there, somewhere, were four more of Plummer's compadres.. He would track them all down and kill them all.

He rose slowly to his feet, unaware of the onlookers, who stood back in awe. He stepped close to Gar Plummer's body and gazed down on it. Strangely, he felt no satisfaction. The same raging hate burned within him. Somehow, even more so. Perhaps the satisfaction would not come until he had wreaked his vengeance on the remaining four.

11

THE DEVIL'S JUSTICE

Ben Slater leaned over the neck of his line back dun as he urged him forward at a continued gallop; slapping him hard with the reins and digging his sharp spurs into the animal's sides, raking them viciously, drawing blood that mixed with the heavy lather already covering the dun's worn out body. Adrenaline flowed rapidly through Slater's veins and sweat from the heat of the New Mexico summer sky dripped into his eyes.

Twice Jace Carlin had crossed his path in the last few months. Once in Tucson and once in Nogales. Slater had heard of Carlin's shooting of Gar Plummer and when Carlin showed up in Tucson, it didn't take much figuring for Slater to assume Carlin was after him, for he had been with Plummer and the others that night they raided the Carlin ranch just north of the Tularosas.. He had kept out of sight by day and by night he waited from a dark alley to catch Carlin alone and by surprise. He had botched the ambush and Carlin had escaped unscathed. Slater had fled from town with Carlin on his tail. It was in Nogales where Carlin caught up with his prey. Slater had escaped once again, but this time a rifle slug from Carlin's Winchester had burned a hole in his side as he fled into the desert. The wound was not serious, but it plagued him with pain and fatigue, constantly slowing him down and allowing Carlin to gain on him.

Jace Carlin, with relentless determination, had followed him for days, across the burning desert and into the jagged Mogollon mountains. Even, here, in the tangled trails and winding canyons, he had not been able to shake his unrelenting pursuer.   He had glimpsed Carlin on his back trail twice in the last half hour. His pursuer was gaining steadily on him as Slater's horse faltered. Now as he forced his weary mount up the steep canyon trail, the line back's front hoofs slipped in the loose shale, sliding under his belly and practically sitting back on his rear haunches. The animal bellowed in torturous pain. Slater's boots slid out of the stirrups and dragged in the loose rock and dirt as horse and rider slid backward, down the bank. The dun shrieked again and his body rolled sideways. Slater leaped from the saddle, fell to the ground, and rolled away from the horse's body as it slid on its side down the embankment, coming to a halt in a pile of shale; his sides expanding and contracting as the animal gasped with hard, labored breaths in the throes of agonizing death.

Slater was momentarily stunned as he lay there, prostrate on the ground, his bearded cheeks half buried in loose rock.   His wound was throbbing and his heart pounded in his head. He didn't hear the steady clip clops of approaching hoofs, at first, but he sensed the impending danger and when he rolled over onto his back he saw the shape of horse and rider looming above him. His eyes squinted, trying to bring the sight into focus and as the blurredness diminished, he saw the menacing stare of Jace Carlin as he sat there, calmly, on his gray mare. Carlin's face was stiff and expressionless. His eyes burned with hate. His lips twisted in a snarl, but no words exuded. He carried his Winchester in his right hand like a pistol and held high. With deliberate coldness, he lowered the barrel.

Slater cringed, digging his back into the shale beneath him. His body shook, anticipating his impending death. Then with desperate resolve, he reached for his six gun as Carlin's rifle exploded. The shot echoed across the canyon and the thrashing line back dun went still and silent with a rifle bullet in its head, putting him out of his misery.

Just as Ben Slater had misread Carlin's action, thinking he was deliberately shooting him without a chance, Jace saw Slater claw for his weapon, and as the recoil of the Winchester subsided, he swung the barrel toward the downed man and fired point blank into his face, splattering blood onto the rocks about him. He lay inert like a pile of dung.

Carlin moved his horse forward, gazing coldly, down at the mass beneath him. This time he did not feel sick as he had with Gar Plummer. In fact, he felt nothing. Not elation, not victory, not regret. Killing was getting easier. But still, satisfaction was absent. Three more he told himself. Then he would be satisfied.

The autumn winds blew cold across the open Kansas prairie. Much too cold for November. Leaves and dust whirled violently about the three riders and their buffalo hide ladened pack mules, as they rode toward the lonely road house that seemed to have been built west of nowhere and still miles from Ellsworth or Wichita.

THE DEVIL'S JUSTICE

The sign outside the ramshackle establishment proclaimed 'Belchers Station- Last stop for food and likker east of Dodge'. The three men, all dressed in thick buffalo hide coats, dismounted and tied their livestock up to the makeshift hitch rail in front of the store and clambered inside.

The place was small and dark inside. Light and wind filtered through the board wall. A heavy plank board had been draped across two barrels, spaced apart to form a make shift bar. The grizzled old store keeper was slumped in a battered wooden chair; one leg shorter than the other three; against the wall at the far end of the bar. He only noted the newcomers with passing interest and remained silent as they sauntered up to the plank, pulling their tattered gloves from their fingers.

"How about some service, here, old man," Dink Marley, the larger of the three men demanded as he pounded on the plank.

"Hold your horses, there, fella," the old man croaked with irritation as he reluctantly got out of his chair and shuffled behind the bar. He retrieved a dusty jug from the shelf and lazily, slammed it on the plank with a thud.

"We don't want any of that slop," Marley boomed. "Ain't you got no good whiskey."

"All I got," the old man said unrattled. "Take it or leave it."

Marley glared at the old man. Then without a word, he lifted the jug, pulled the cork with his teeth, spit it out on the plank, and began to guzzle straight from the jug.

THE DEVIL'S JUSTICE

"Hey. Wait a minute, there, Dink," one of his companion, Ike Soames complained. "Save some for us." He placed both hands around the jug and jerked it away from Marley. "Ain't you got no manners?"

Marley wiped the excess liquid that dripped from his full beard with the sleeve of his coat. "Well don't you two go drinkin' it all," he complained.

Soames had chugged several large gulps before the third man snatched the jug away and attacked it hungrily. "Save enough for me. I need another shot."

"I'll oblige you with another shot," a level voice sounded behind them. Cold wind had rushed through the store as the shadowed figure of a man stepped into the open doorway; the light of day backlighting him. He stepped forward slowly and the glancing light filtering between loose boards of the wall half revealed the man's face.

Marley froze as if in a trance. Even in the dim light, he recognized Jace Carlin. He had heard what had happened to Gar Plummer and Ben Slater. Jace Carlin had been garnering a huge reputation and his skill with a gun was becoming well known. Word had spread across the frontier of Carlin's quest for vengeance against the men that had killed his family. Marley took a deep breath and held it. Then let it out slowly, accepting the fact that Carlin had finally found him. "I'm not gonna let this be easy for you, Carlin," he said, pushing the right side of his coat tail back, exposing the big navy revolver in his holster.

THE DEVIL'S JUSTICE

"Doesn't matter much to me," Carlin said evenly; his fingers curled above his pistol handle.

"You'll have to take me too, Mister," Soames warned, stepping away from Marley and pushing his coat aside to reveal a battered ball and cap pistol snugged in a left sided holster in a right hand cross draw position.

"I'm not here for you, Mister," Carlin warned. "Best you don't mix in to somethin' that don't concern you." He had hardly said the words, when both men went for their guns.

Calmly, swiftly, and surely, Jace Carlin pulled his revolver, thumbing back the hammer as he drew. The weapon belched and the first slug caught Marley squarely in the chest, where his open coat had revealed his dirty shirt. Marley's eyes bulged with surprise. His pistol was only half out of its holster and he bent forward in stiffening pain.

Carlin shifted the gun muzzle slightly to the left and the weapon sounded again; a deafening roar in the confines of the wooden structure, even before the thunder of the first shot had died away. Soames felt the slug tear into his middle and fell back against the plank bar.

His first shot at Marley had been a bit hasty, as he needed to answer the other man drawing against him. Carlin, then, swung his pistol barrel back toward Marley and shot him two more times as his body slumped to the floor. In the same split second he aimed back to the other man and fired again as he was still falling.

The third man with Marley and Soames, had stepped back away from his two companions. He was cringing with fear and both of his arms were held high in the air. "Please, Mister," he begged. "I don't want any part of this."

"Too bad that other fella wasn't as smart," Carlin said striding forward and examining the bodies. "My quarrel was with Marley, not him." He holstered his pistol, turned and walked out into the cold prairie wind.

The Montana snow had hit early and hard this year. The winds blew with a fierceness off the Tetons and the bitter cold chilled man and beast to the bone. Anyone with any sense would find a place to hole up until the weather broke. But Al Drago was scared. When Jace Carlin rode into Billings the day before, Drago knew what he was there for. He had heard about the deaths of three former companions and knew that he, Drago, was the next target of the avenging manhunter.

He had retrieved his horse from the livery in the middle of the night and had ridden out into the harsh winter with no place to go except away from Carlin's wrath. Drago had headed into the mountains, hoping to get through the passes before they piled too high with snow. With any luck, he would make it through leaving Carlin snowed in behind him.

The wind whipped through his sheepskin coat as if it was paper and his hat was tied down under his chin with his scarf, to keep it in place and cover his ears. Snow and ice spicules pelted his eyes fiercely, forcing them to squint almost shut, as he trudged onward into the night.

THE DEVIL'S JUSTICE

His horse kept bogging down to his haunches in the drifting snow and from time to time, Drago would have to dismount and try to lead the horse forward. He had been traveling for several hours, now. Dawn should be coming soon, but in the midst of blizzard, no sign of morning light could be discerned.

He had been leading the horse for quite sometime now and with every step they took, they both sank deeper and deeper in the piling white stuff. Every step became a bigger challenge. Each step took greater effort and man and beast both sucked cold air into their lungs. Deeper and deeper the snow drifted until it seemed as if the next step would bury them. It was no use to continue with the horse. Drago dropped the reins and crawled forward through the snow until exhaustion over came him. He finally let himself sink into the snow and lay quiet, save for his laboring breath. He was giving up, knowing that to do so would mean freezing to death.

The snow began to pile over him and he drifted off to sleep.

Dawn crept over the mountains and the wind quieted. The blizzard was subsiding and the darkness became a pale gray. The snow had drifted over Al Drago and had insulated him from the cold wind. By some strange miracle, he had not yet frozen to death. He began to awaken and stirred, snow falling from his covered body, as he forced himself to rise and roll over.

Even the pale light of early morning, seemed bright to him, after a night of almost total darkness. Elation began to sweep over him as he realized he was still alive. But that sudden excitement faded as fast as it had arrived as he looked up into the menacing eyes of a man, wearing snow shoes, standing above him. Jace Carlin pointed the muzzle of his Winchester directly at Drago's chest. Drago tried to speak. To plead for his life, but his throat was too tight to make a sound.

Carlin had not a word to utter. His face was as cold as the Montana winter. Expressionless, and void of any emotion. Drago stared blankly up at the man and thought he should be trembling; wondering why he wasn't. The realization that he was going to die on this godforsaken mountain, whether by a bullet or freezing out there in the wilderness, swept over him and he accepted it with serene resolve. His snow covered eyelids drooped in defeat for a moment, then in a split second of reckless abandonment, he rolled to his side, grasping for the pistol on his hip beneath his coat.

Carlin saw the movement, and without hesitation or remorse, he squeezed the trigger of his rifle. The bullet drilled through Drago's right hand and tore into his thick coat. Drago's body fell back into the snow; his chest blossoming in crimson liquid, that dripped into the pure white snow beneath him.

Carlin ejected the shell from his rifle and strode away without looking back.

The little town of Clairmont was unusually busy for a weekday. With the coming of spring, farmers and homesteader had come to town to gather the necessary supplies and seed needed for planting season.

Kurt Egstrom was a big man of thirty. Tall and thick, yet not an ounce of fat on him. He had neatly trimmed blond hair and blue eyes. Everything about him proclaimed his Swedish decent except for his speech, which was very clear without a hint of accent. His powerful shoulders carried the sacks of seed easily as he loaded his wagon in front of the general store.

"That's the lot of them, Aggie," he said to his wife as he stacked the last sack in place, filling up the wagon bed. "I'll have a lot of planting to do." He glanced up at the early spring sky.

"Can I help, this year, Pa?" The ten year old boy beside him said.

"Sure you can, Billy. It's time you started learning to do a man's work." He tossled the boy's light hair with his calloused, rough fingers; smiling with pride at his boy. He was feeling good, happy with his wife and son and looking forward to the prospect of a new year's crop.

"Oh, Kurt," Aggie said. "Can't you let him be a little boy, just a while longer?"

"I don't want to be a little boy, no more, Ma," Billy protested.

"The boy's right, Aggie," Kurt said. "It's about time that......" His words trailed off. The smile on his lips faded and his face paled as he looked down the street and saw the man walking in the middle of it; coming his way.

Kurt swallowed hard and felt a lump in his throat. The hairs on the back of his neck stood up and a cold chill ran down his spine. Somehow, he had told himself, that this day would never come. He never believed he had been responsible for what had happened, so long ago. He had merely been with the other men. He hadn't been a part of it, but yes, he knew he was guilty. Guilty of allowing it to happen. Yet he told himself, he was only one man and there were four others. How could he have stopped them? He couldn't have. But, he could've tried. For that he was guilty. And for letting the others ride off free without reporting them to the law.

As Kurt Egstrom watched Jace Carlin come closer, he thought of how he would have felt if it had happened to his family instead of Carlin's. He would probably be doing just what Carlin was doing right now. Seeking out and destroying the men responsible. He looked from Carlin to Aggie and Billy.

"What...what is it, Kurt," Aggie asked, suddenly pulling Billy close to her. "Do you know that man?"

"Take Billy and go back inside the store, Aggie," he ordered flatly without answering her question and not taking his eyes off the approaching man. She hesitated. Wanted to say something, but Kurt added without looking at her or Billy. "Go on. Do as I say."

Egstrom moved slowly and deliberately to the front of his wagon, reached under the seat, and retrieved an old Remington long barreled revolver. He stepped away from the rig, into the middle of the street; his right arm hanging heavily, straight down, holding the big weapon tightly in his fist. He spread his legs shoulder width apart and waited for Carlin to come closer, within earshot. Eternally long moments ticked by. Carlin strode steadily closer. Close enough now.

"I'm sorry about your family," Egstrom shouted. There was a trace of tremble in his voice. "I didn't want it to happen. It was the others."

Carlin halted a moment. "You were there." Carlin proclaimed coldly, then continued forward.

"Yes. I...I was," Kurt answered. "I couldn't stop them. What else could I do?" He didn't expect a reply nor did the approaching gunman one offer one. He just kept coming.

His legs felt numb and his massive body trembled. He raised his Remington to shoulder level, his arm outstretched and his sighted the weapon straight at Carlin. Carlin never altered nor slackened his step; just kept advancing.

"Carlin!" A deep voice boomed from behind Carlin and off to his right.

Jace halted, glancing furtively toward the warning voice; but still keeping Egstrom in view.

A lean figure stepped of the plank sidewalk into the street. A pistol was in hand and it was aimed directly at Carlin. The man was a bit stooped with age, but he had probably been tall in his younger years. Gray temples protruded beneath a Derby black hat that matched his black linen suit. A star proclaiming him town marshal was pinned to his lapel.

"I'll have none of this in my town, Carlin," the Marshal warned. "You too, Kurt," he added. "Put your weapon away."

Jace turned his attention back to Egstrom. Off to the left, in the doorway of the general store, he could see Egstrom's wife holding her son close and watching.

Kurt maintained his stance; pistol still aimed at Carlin. "Sorry, Asa," was his answer to the town marshal. "Can't let it go." He eared back the hammer and tightened his finger on the trigger, taking up slack.

"Don't be a fool, Kurt," Asa warned. "You're no gunfighter. He'll kill you."

Sweat was beading on Kurt's forehead and his palms were moist, throat dry.

"Put the gun away, Kurt," the Marshal pleaded. "If you don't fight, there's nothing he can do short of murder. He won't do that."

"Don't count on it law dog," Carlin warned coldly, without taking his eyes off the Swede.

"Listen to Asa, Kurt," Aggie called from behind. Kurt stiffened, feeling her fear.

"Sorry, Aggie," Kurt answered. He wanted to turn and look at her one last time, but he couldn't take his eyes off Carlin. "If I don't face him now, he'll only follow us home. Asa has no jurisdiction there. He can't help us. No. I'd rather do it here and now where everyone can see it."

"Why, Kurt? Why is he after you? What could you have possibly done to him?" Aggie sobbed.

"I'm afraid it's what I didn't do," Kurt answered with resolve, then stepped forward toward Carlin, pushing the weapon straight out ahead of him as he walked.

"No Kurt," Asa warned sharply.

"Keep out of it, Asa!" Kurt answered. "I've got to do this." Then without breaking stride, he squeezed the trigger. Jace Carlin felt the sting as the slug tore a chip out of the top of his left ear and he flinched, but the cold expression on his face never changed. He kept his eyes on Egstrom, watching the big man come closer and cocking his pistol to fire again. Carlin casually lifted his hand and felt the gash. Warm blood trickled onto his finger tips.

Egstrom's weapon boomed again. This time the bullet ripped Carlin's upper right arm and burned a scratch across the meaty part of his muscle. Again the gunman flinched, but didn't move.

Egstrom kept coming, thumbing back the hammer again. He was close enough now that Carlin could hear it click to full cock.

This time Jace Carlin didn't let the big Swede fire again. Effortlessly, he slid his own six shooter from its holster and fired.

Kurt Egstrom stiffened; his eyes wide in surprise. He bent at the waist and started to fall. Carlin fired again, catching the big man in the chest, straightening him upward and throwing him back under the impact of the .45 calibre slug. He landed hard on his back. Dust from the street beneath him billowed up around him and drifted down over his lifeless body.

"Noooooooo!" Aggie screamed, running into the street and dropping to her knees next to her fallen husband. Billy ran after her, big tears streaming down his round cheeks.

Carlin sheathed his weapon, watching the scene before him. The hysterical woman cradling her husband's head in her arms, rocking back and forth, sobbing. The little boy clinging to his mother, arms wrapped about her neck from behind. His face buried in the softness of her hair, soaking it with tears. His mother, so consumed with grief, seemed not to notice. The boy, feeling alone and abandoned lifted his head and glared at Jace Carlin through his streaming tears.

"I hate you!" He shouted angrily. "You've killed my pa. You're a bad man. I hate you. You hear me? I hate you. When I grow up, I'm gonna find you and I'm gonna kill you just like you did my pa." He buried his face back into his mother's hair.

For the first time in a long time, the coldness in Jace Carlin seemed to thaw. He felt something he had forgotten for a long time. The haunting strains of regret. Remorse? No. It can't be. He remembered his own grief and tried not to wonder if this was what Egstrom's family was feeling. He remembered his own hate and could see it in this enraged, confused little boy. The boy, who reminded him so much of his own boy. His son, who he would never see grow up. His anger returned and he told himself he had done what he had to do. He had set out for satisfaction and now he had found it. He had tracked them all down, now. He had avenged his family. Yes, he was satisfied, he told himself. But, why did he feel so empty? So wrong?

The town marshal stepped up beside Carlin. His gun was still in his hand.

"He fired first, Marshal," Jace said, still watching Egstrom's family. "You saw it."

THE DEVIL'S JUSTICE

"Yes, I saw it," the Marshal said with a sigh. His voice was gravelly. "There's nothing I can hold you for, so best you mount up and ride out of town before I can think of something."

Carlin eyed him levelly. "No problem. I got what I came for." He started to turn and walk away.

"And what did you come for?" Asa asked. "Vengeance?"

Jace halted and turned. "No, Marshal," he said flatly. "I came for justice."

"Justice?" Asa said, nodding toward the Egstrom's. "I've heard about you and your so called justice. Call it what you want, but I call it vengeance. And vengeance is the devil's justice. Remember that. And I hope you're satisfied."

Carlin looked him straight in the eye. "I'm satisfied," he said. Then he turned and walked away.

THE DEVIL'S JUSTICE

Chapter Two

The mid morning sun loomed as a huge shimmering orb just above the crest of the hill; its rays protruding long fingers against the pale blue sky. A shadow emerged from the other side of the hill. A horse and rider, just a slow moving black dot against the brilliant light.

Jace Carlin reined the gray mare to a halt and sat quietly, looking down into the valley below. He took a deep breath, smelling the dampness of the early morning mist. The air was crisp and sounds of the town below drifted clearly upwards. The clang of a blacksmith's hammer against an anvil. Storekeepers opening their doors and cranking out awnings. The clatter of boot steps against the plank sidewalks. The creak of wagon wheels as locals traversed the streets of Contention Springs.

The town was very much the same as it was when Jace had left it four years ago. Four years, Jace thought to himself. Is that all it's been? Yet, it seemed like a lifetime ago, since he had ridden out of this valley on his quest for vengeance against the men that had taken his family from him. Vengeance? He thought. Yes, he had finally come to terms with what it really was. He had told himself for so long that it was justice, but the old lawman's words had followed him these past few months. "Vengenace is the Devil's Justice." The memory of a woman and little boy grieving over a man he had taken from them, had plagued his days and haunted his dreams.

When he rode out of Clairmont that fateful day, he thought he had finally wreaked retribution on the ones who had taken his very life and existence from him; leaving him empty inside with no purpose in life. The vengeance trail had given him a purpose; seek out and destroy. And, he had done that. But the emptiness was still there.

He had barely ridden out of town when he suddenly became aware that he knew not where he was headed. For the first time in a long time, he had no purpose. No trails to follow. No desperadoes to track down. No where to go. He shouldn't feel this way, he told himself. He had gotten his satisfaction and the long hunt was over. Over! What would he do now? He forced the thought to the back of his mind. He told himself that he was just tired. Perhaps he should camp for the night. Rest. Think about what he was going to do next. Where to go.

He had camped in a grove of junipers next to a stream. Sleep did not come easy to him and several times he climbed out of his blankets and paced around the camp. He sat on a rock next to the babbling stream, feeling the briskness of the night air, listening to night sounds and occasionally slapping at mosquitoes.

It was past midnight, when he finally fell to exhaustion and went to sleep. But the sleep had been fitful and his brain filled with tormenting images. That night in pouring rain as he lay wounded next to his brother, Josh. Poor Josh. He had never had a chance in life. With only the mental capacity of a child, he had grown to a man of complete innocence. A naiveté that the rest of the world lacked and could not understand. Jace had taken care of him ever since their parents died of Cholera when they were just kids. Jace and his brother had come west on a wagon train several years ago. It was when the train stopped over in Contention Springs, that Jace met Jenna and Alice Shaw. He decided to leave the train and settle in the basin east of Contention Springs. Here, he and his brother built a log cabin and began ranching. Josh had worked hard alongside his brother and the ranch grew to a sizeable spread and a large herd. It was just a year later that Jace married Alice and the year after that their son was born.

Life had been good for the Carlin's until that night when five riders rode down on them.

In his dreams, Jace could hear the pounding of hoofs, the drunken shouts and laughter of riders and the roar of sixguns. He could see the engulfing flames of his house and the screams of his family inside. Jace tossed in his blankets, feeling his helplessness; seeing himself lying in the mud, rain pelting his face, while unable to move. Unable to save his family. Unable to fight back.

Once again he looked into the flames. This time he saw Egstrom's wife and little boy; burning rafters falling on them, consuming them. The boy's face loomed large in the flames. He screamed, "I hate you! You killed my Pa! When I grow up, I'll kill you.!"

The attacking marauders continued to circle the burning cabin, on their mounts. Their guns

THE DEVIL'S JUSTICE

blazed in the darkness and the thunder of horses hooves were muted by the slosh of thick mud. And as each rider loomed before Carlin's fallen body, he heard their hideous laughing and saw their evil, twisted faces. And each one's face was the face of Jace Carlin, himself.

Carlin had jerked himself awake, sweat streaming down his face in icy fingers as the chill of the near dawn air quickly dried them and left him cold as a corpse.

Night after night the dreams returned and each day started with the same coldness. Day after day, Jace Carlin saddled up and rode on to nowhere, trying to decide what to do, where to go. The days grew long and endless. Only the sound of the mare's hoofs sounding in his ears. The sound of gunfire and screams of a woman and a boy echoed in his brain. He saw men dying before his avenging gun and the lights going out of their eyes as they died.

From time to time Carlin had drifted into a town. He tried to sleep in a bed, but the dreams persisted, just as they had on the trail. He tried to wash away the memories with whiskey, but that didn't work either. To make matters worse, in each town, he found that he had garnered a reputation and there were men itching to best him. Two more gunnies had died before Carlin's gun, before Jace decided to stay away from towns and people.

For days he stayed in the mountains and badlands; alone save for the haunting memories that continually consumed him. The days turned into weeks and then a month. There was still no where to go and no purpose left in his life. Then one early dawn, he awoke from his sleep and realized that, either through sheer exhaustion or some divine providence, he had slept the night through dreamless. As his eyes slowly opened, washing the sleep away, shimmering fingers of gold and orange against a red tinged clear blue sky lifted above the far horizon. He felt the warmth of the rising sun cover him like a blanket and soothing the chill in his soul. As if a messenger from heaven had awakened him and had given him an answer. Jace Carlin arose from his blankets, broke camp, and saddled up. As he started to mount, a thought crossed his mind. He stepped down and unbuckled his gun belt. He tossed the rig, pistol and all onto the ground and let it lie where it fell. A wisp of dust blew over it as he turned to mount. He hesitated, thinking of the men in various towns who had braced him. As much as he no longer wanted to use a gun, the nagging thought of being caught defenseless, gave him pause. Then thinking better of it, he reached down and retrieved the holster and gun. He wrapped the belt tightly around them and tucked it all away in his saddle bag. Just in case, he thought, though he hoped he would never have a need for weapons again. Then he swung into the saddle, turning the mare to the north and gigged her forward. He was going home.

And, now as he slouched in the saddle, looking down at the town below, he began to question if he had been right in coming back. The pit of his stomach twisted into a hard knot and ached. Memories flooded his brain. He could see himself with Alice, little Joey and Josh loading their wagon in front of the general store. He could hear their laughter. He remembered barn dances and barbeques with the neighbors. He saw them all in the comfort of their home in the basin and he felt the warmth of all the good times they had. A tear started at the corner of his eye and he brushed it away quickly, fighting back the urge to cry. Then it all faded as the memories of that fateful night pushed the happy images from sight. His jaw set hard and grimness returned to his stubbled youthful face.

"Well old girl," he said to the mare. "We've come this far. I reckon, I'd be somewhat of a coward if I turned back now. Lord knows I'm scared though. I sure hope I'm doing the right thing." He looked up at the sky as if seeking more answers. A few clouds hung motionless in the otherwise empty blue sky. This time, there was no messenger, no warmth of assurance. Just the chill of what might lie ahead.

Then with a sigh of resignation, he lifted the reins, touched his spurs gently against the mare's flanks and guided her down the slope into the main street of Contention Springs.

From his vantage point, on the hill above town, it did not appear that much had changed in this little cow town while he had been away, but as he entered the main street and could see it up close, he saw that much had indeed changed. The town appeared shabbier than what he had remembered. Many of the establishments were in need of repair and paint. There were several businesses that had closed up. Windows and doors had been boarded shut; their owners obviously had packed up and left. The Lucky 7 Saloon, further down the street to the right was still open, but this too was not as he had remembered it. Unlike the rest of the town, it was not in disrepair. It sported a wildly outlandish lavender paint job. An addition had been added to the far side, providing for a garishly designed hotel, with ornate pillars. Its new coat of white paint gleamed in the morning sun.

Across the street from the Lucky 7 was another saloon. This was a new structure that had been built since Carlin had been away. The brightly painted sign over the bat wing doors was emblazoned with the words 'Lady Luck Emporium.' Like its competitor across the street it appeared to be a prosperous enterprise.

Jace kept his head down, hoping the brim of his hat would conceal his face, somewhat, as he rode slowly along the street. His eyes darted back and forth, looking for familiar faces. There seemed to be many new people in town. That lifted his spirits a bit. Maybe, his apprehension about retuning to old friends and neighbors had bee ill founded. But, that elation was short lived as he recognized familiar faces. Les Sturgis, the village blacksmith had lifted the hot horseshoe from his anvil and was dipping it in the cooling water trough. It sizzled and steamed into the crisp morning air. His massive, shaggy head jerked up suddenly as he recognized Jace Carlin passing by.

Jace noticed him staring, but continued to ride forward, without slackening the mare's pace.

THE DEVIL'S JUSTICE

He tried to appear to be looking straight ahead and seeing nothing to either side.

The blacksmith stood stock still; his stare following the rider as the horse's hoofs clip clopped past him.

Time seemed to slow down to a crawl for Jace Carlin, and he forced down the urge to hurry the mare along. As he rode further on he passed Sy Miller, standing on the porch of his general store. Across the street, Bill Payson was rolling out the awning in front of his tonsorial parlor. He stopped his cranking, jaw slack in surprise, as he watched Jace pass by.

Off to his right, he passed the local newspaper; The Contention Clarion. Like many of the other buildings, it had a shabbiness about it that had not been there before. It had been a prosperous paper and its editor and publisher, John Parker had been a visionary and a leading citizen for Contention Springs. The morning sun glanced off the plate glass window, painting the image of the street and the passing rider across it. Inside, eyes peered though the glass, totally hidden from the outside by the sun's reflections. The eyes were large and clear blues. They watched intently as the rider passed by. Amy Parker pushed back a wisp of her light brown hair from her slender young face. She wiped her hands against her printer's apron, smoothing it out and then absently pushing her hair back, although it was tied tightly in a bun just above the nape of her neck.

Across the street, Will Parmelee stepped through the doorway of the Sheriff's Office onto the board sidewalk. He was a tall, lean man, in his early thirties, with broad shoulders and narrow hips. His dark eyes squinted against the bright morning sunlight, but it didn't prevent him from noticing Carlin pass by. A five pointed star was pinned to the left side of Parmelee's brown leather vest. He stepped out into the middle of the street, feet spread apart and thumbs hooked in his gunbelt. He stared at Carlin's retreating back and his craggy face turned to stone. Trouble had come to town.

Carlin angled his mount to the left and reined up in front of the Contention Springs Hotel. This too looked a bit run down as if business had fallen off like the rest of the town's commercial establishments. The faded sign outside still proclaimed Ethan Decker as owner and proprietor.

Jace stepped down from the saddle and tied the reins to the hitch rail. As he secured the slip knot, he glanced up and back along the street. His glance lingered as he recognized Will Parmalee crossing the street and stepping onto the sidewalk in front of the newspaper office. Amy Parker had stepped out of the building to greet him, warmly. He had put his hands on her arms and they were both looking in Carlin's direction. Presently, John Parker came through the doorway to join them. The newspaper man looked much older than Jace had remembered him. His shoulders were stooped and his otherwise dark hair was almost gray now. He too was looking in Jace's direction. Obviously, Jace was the object of conversation. Not that he was surprised, but he had hoped to be less conspicuous. He was not yet ready to renew old acquaintances and tried to act as if he was unaware of the attention he was drawing.

He untied the thongs behind his saddle and removed his saddlebags. The extra weight they carried, reminded him he still had his gun. He tossed the bags over his shoulder and started toward the hotel entrance.

"Jace! Jace Carlin!" he heard a voice shouting behind him. It was Parmalee's. Carlin paused in front of the door. He almost started again, as if ignoring the call. But he thought better of it and decided to meet the situation head on. He sighed and gritted his teeth. With a turn in place, he watched Parmalee hurrying across the street toward him, his long legs lengthening his strides.

There was a little extra breathiness in his voice, from the quickened pace as he reached Carlin, extending his hand in greeting. "This is a surprise, Jace," he said cordially with a smile, but his eyes reflected a certain wariness. "Been a long time."

Jace reluctantly took the man's hand and shook it, albeit not with enthusiasm. He nodded toward the star on Parmalee's vest. "Still Deputy Sheriff, I see," Jace acknowledged.

"Not exactly," Will responded, lifting the frock of his vest so the star could be more visible. "It's Sheriff, now." There was a flatness to his voice as he said it.

Jace looked the lawman up and down, coolly. "Well, congratulations, Will. What happened to Russ Shaw. He was still Sheriff when I left."

THE DEVIL'S JUSTICE

"Russ retired shortly after…" He didn't finish. "You know after what happened. Right after you rode out."

"Right after I rode out to do his job," Carlin stated. "Your's too." He leveled his gaze steely at Will.

Will's forehead furrowed. "I was only his deputy, Jace. He ordered me not to intervene. He was afraid what would happen to the town, if we tried to take them. He was an old man, Jace. Long past his prime. He never thought he would ever have to stand up against men like them."

"Well, he didn't," Carlin retorted bitterly.

"And he was sorry. He never got over it. Afterall, Alice was his daughter. He never got over it."

'Neither did I," Jace started to turn away.

"What brings you back?" Parmalee raised his voice authoritatively. It was a command for answer rather than a question for conversation.

Jace leveled his gaze into Parmalee's. "It's my home," he almost growled evenly. "Is there a problem with that, Sheriff?" the emphasis was on 'Sheriff'.

Will splayed both hands, patting the air defensively. "Hold on there, Jace," he said. "I meant no harm. I just wanted to greet you back, is all. I had hoped you had gotten over your bitterness."

"Me too, Will," Jace said in a softer tone almost apologetically. "I'm trying. You just caught me a little off guard. I'm sorry." Then he added as if he knew what the lawman really was concerned about. "You have no worry about me. I

THE DEVIL'S JUSTICE

want no trouble. "I'm trying to put that all behind me now."

Parmalee nodded. A slight half smile. "We all heard about you, Jace. How you tracked them all down. You've made a reputation for yourself."

"Don't worry, Will. I'm not bringing trouble with me. I've put away my gun."

"I noticed," the Sheriff said. "You think that's wise? There's always going to be someone looking to build a rep for themselves. What will you do without a gun?"

"I guess I could die and you'd have the honor of hanging the gent that did it." He forced a smile and Will returned it.

"Well let's hope it doesn't come to that, Jace," the lawman said. Then he added, still probing. "So you plan on living here again?"

"That's right. It's time I started over. I have a good spread. I made it pay before. I can do it again."

"You'll have a lot of memories to deal with, Jace. Are you sure you're up to it?"

"I don't know. I hope so. At least I can try."

"Might be easier if you tried to start somewhere fresh and new," Parmalee said.

"It might," Carlin agreed. "But I have land here, already. I just don't have the money to buy elsewhere. Besides, my family is buried here. I belong here."

"You've been gone a long time, Jace. You haven't worked that land for four years. Thing's have changed around here since you left."

"Changed? How?"

THE DEVIL'S JUSTICE

"Well...." Parmalee stammered with avoidance. "What I'm saying is that time changes things. That's all. I just think you might be better off elsewhere."

"Is that a warning, Sheriff?" Carlin's round eyes narrowed and edginess returned to his voice.

"No. No, of course not, Jace. I'm just concerned. We are still friends aren't we?"

Carlin eyed the man up and down. "Sure," he said flatly, turned and entered the hotel, leaving Parmalee standing in the street.

Sweat dripped off Jace Carlin's round chin. He used the tips of the loose hanging bandana from around his neck to wipe his face. The early afternoon sun was burning hot and Carlin had been keeping to the shade of trees along the trail as he rode out of the hills and into the basin where his ranch was located. As he sat astride his mount at the rim of the basin, his eyes searched the far expanse that he had once called home.

Knowing, he would have a great deal of work to do before he could move back to his home spread, Jace Carlin had taken a room in the hotel. After cleaning up a bit and stabling the mare, treating her to fresh oats and a rubdown, Jace had taken lunch at the only café in town. Business was light and he was glad that he hadn't run into anyone he knew. Even the cook and waitress were new to him. The management had obviously changed hands while he was away.

He stayed away from the counter and found a small table in a far corner of the room. He draped his Stetson over the back of the chair opposite and he sat with his back to the rest of the room. He had ordered a hot roast beef sandwich and some coffee and was just finishing when he sensed, rather than saw, the shadow or presence of someone standing behind him. He turned slowly and warily, although sensing that danger was not eminent.

His expression was one of surprise, though not unsuspecting. His tanned face paled and he felt a chill, choking back any reaction that might reveal the tinge of excitement he felt as he saw Amy Parker standing there.

"Hello, Jace," she said softly. She no longer wore her printer's apron, but there was an ink smudge on the left shoulder of her blue gingham dress and a spot of ink under her chin. Amy had been a good friend of his wife in the old days; although she had been much younger than Alice. The two of them had been very close. Alice regarded her as a younger sister; something that Alice's own sister, Jenna, had always resented.

"Hello, Amy," Jace smiled warmly. "You certainly have grown up," he said admiringly.

Her face flushed a bit, but she passed over the comment, which she took as a compliment. "Mind if I join you?" She said, already moving to a chair, readying to sit down.

"No. No. Of course not," he said, knowing he really didn't have any choice.

"Glad to see you're back," Amy attempted conversation, not quite sure how to start.

Jace smiled. "I hope I'm glad too," he said, swiveling in his chair to face her on the opposite side of the table.

THE DEVIL'S JUSTICE

"You don't know?" Amy asked.

"Sorry, I don't. Not sure if it's going to work out. Not sure if anyone around here even wants me back."

"Oh sure," she smiled. "All of your old friends will be glad."

"I'm not so sure. I didn't get the impression that Will Parmelee wants me here. And I'm sure Russ Shaw won't be happy to hear I'm back."

"Will's your friend, Jace. He's just concerned about you. As for Russ Shaw, he's a sick old man. I'm sure he's more concerned about you having a grudge against him."

"Well, if I have," Jace said. "I'm going to try not to keep it. I've had enough revenge." His eyes saddened. "Too much in fact. And I'm only the worse for it. It didn't bring my family back."

"I'm sorry, Jace," she answered, not knowing what else to say.

"I know," he responded. Then changed the subject. "So tell me. Are you and Randy Poole married yet?"

She lowered her lashes and took a deep breath. She felt like she was blurting it out. "No. Randy's dead."

Carlin bolted upright, surprise on his face.

She continued. "We were to be married, but he was killed a year and a half ago."

"I'm so sorry, Amy. What...what happened? How?"

Amy reached for the words, her hands wringing.

"But if you don't want to talk about, you don't have...."

THE DEVIL'S JUSTICE

She cut him off. "No. No that's alright. I can talk about it."

He waited a moment. Then she started. "You know he was working for Duncan Holt."

Carlin nodded. Duncan Holt had been one of Jace's best friends. He owned the spread to the East of Carlin's and was married to Alice's sister Jenna.

"There are new owners on Ben Crenshaw's old place to the west and south of you. It's called the Diamond 8 now. They claimed Duncan was rustling their herds, but it was just an excuse to bring in hired guns and try to take over the other ranches in the valley. They claimed the Rafter h was stealing cattle and one day Randy was found shot to death. Of course they denied it,but there was no reason for anyone else to kill Randy., He didn't have an enemy in the world. You know that."

"Yes, I do," Jace muttered. Then he said. "What about Will Parmalee? Couldn't he do anything about it?"

She shook her head. "No. There were no witness, There was nothing Will could do."

"Or maybe, he didn't want to," Carlin mused bitterly.

"That's not fair, Jace."

"You seem real touchy about Will, Amy. Looked to me like you two are real chummy, when I saw you out there on the street."

Amy's eyes flashed and she pushed herself up from the chair. "Yes. Yes we are. It's none of your business, but Will and I are going to be married next month. I...I thought we were all friends, but I guess you've changed too much for that." She stomped away and slammed the café door as she went out.

He felt a pang of guilt as he watched her go. Maybe he had changed too much.

Now as he sat in the saddle above the basin, he admitted that perhaps things had changed, as Will Parmalee had warned. He had expected his ranch to be overgrown with weeds from neglect. He had expected to see the ruins of his cabin, but this was not the case. Where his cabin had once stood, the ground had been laid bare and grass now grew in its place. Gone was any trace of his barn, corral and other outbuildings. His eyes searched frantically for signs of the little cemetery where his family had been laid to rest. No markers existed. An emptiness settled into the pit of his stomach and it ached. It was almost as if his home and family had never existed. In its place was rolling rangeland, full of lush grass and cattle dotting the range for miles. But whose cattle were they?

Could it be that he had ridden the wrong way? That he had forgotten his way to his own home and was looking at the wrong basin? No! He could not persuade himself that such was the case. Someone had taken over his land. Was this why Will Parmalee wanted him to ride on? Had he been afraid of Carlin's reaction, when he found he had lost his home? Maybe so, Jace acknowledged to himself. He was feeling the familiar rage building inside him. He remembered the men who had died before his gun and he fought to restrain himself. Whatever had happened here, he had to change it without violence.

THE DEVIL'S JUSTICE

He rode down into the basin and guided his horse in among the grazing cattle. At first he saw no brands. Then he realized he was among young stock that had not yet been branded. He looked around for older stock with a brand that would tell him who the cattle belonged to. He picked out a rangy old mossey horn grazing on a knoll a short distance away and pricked his spurs to the mare's sides, urging her up the incline.

He was stepping out of the saddle almost before the mare slid to a complete stop. The mossey horn shied quickly away. Carlin slowed his approach and stepped gently in a half circle toward and around the animal until he could see the brand. Diamond 8!

He almost lost his balance as something hissed through the air over his head. The surprise was such that he did not readily realize that a hemp lariat had looped above him and had dropped over his head, settling around his shoulders and drawing his arms tight to his sides and pulled him sideways, off his feet. He felt the ground rush up to meet him. Pain racked down his left side and the fall drove breath from his lungs. And then he felt himself moving; sliding, twisting and turning; finally realizing that he was being dragged behind a galloping horse.

THE DEVIL'S JUSTICE

Chapter Three

Grass, sky and sunlight whipped past Carlin in blinding, confused, chaotic shards of blue, green, and bright light. He twisted sharply in the confines of the taught rope, trying to regain some modicum of control over his body and pull his head erect enough and steady enough to focus his vision and to see more than mere flashes of color and light. His range hat, which had been tied beneath his chin, slipped off and the string stretched tight across his throat. The hat flopped about his shoulders and back and whipped at his face, pelting his eyes.

The grass and hard pack beneath him scraped at his body, pulling his shirt loose from beneath his belt until his skin was exposed. The rough terrain then dug deeper into his hide and blood appeared from the many scratches and his body bruised as it slid over rocks and stones.

It seemed as if he had been dragged for miles, with the pounding of horse's hoofs in front of him. Desperately, he fought at the rope. The struggle just made the pain and abrasions worse, but he twisted violently left and right until he managed to pull himself flat on his stomach, reaching up with both hands from under the loop to grasp the rope ahead of him. The skin on his underside burned fiercely as he pulled his upper body up, lifting his shoulders off the ground enough to look along the rope and see the horse and rider ahead of him. Off to the side, out of the corner of his eye, he could see another rider coming along side of him, whipping a coiled rope at him. He twisted away just as the rider swung the hard coil and barely missed his head as he moved. But, as the rider ahead loosed the rope, allowing Carlin to slide to an abrupt stop, Carlin rolled back just enough for the next arc of the coiled rope to whack him hard in the back of the head, beating his face into the grass.

Carlin's body went limp and he lay there stunned, breathing hard, almost unconscious, yet just enough awake to be aware of the two men dismounting and rushing to his side. He felt big hands on his shoulders and then felt himself being pulled erect on his feet. His legs were of rubber and he would have slumped back to the ground if he hadn't been held in place. Carlin's head raised just enough to see a big burly man with a flaming red beard before him. The man's huge fist grew enormous as it came straight into his face. His head felt as if it had exploded with a flash of lightning and intermittent darkness. The man behind him held him steady as the blow plowed into Carlin's left jaw. His head jerked to the side and blood oozed from the corner of his mouth.

In one smooth motion, the man holding him, spun him around in place and Carlin fell into the arms of red beard. His eyes opened just enough to see a rangy black stubbled face before him. His fist loomed just as huge as red beard's and slammed into his face. Carlin's head, once again, whipped to the side. This time total darkness washed over him and he felt him self slumping freely to the ground, before succumbing to total unconsciousness.

The hot afternoon sun paled into a round yellow ball against the light blue sky, spreading its warmth over the lone, still figure, lying flat on his back, in the grassland below.

Jace Carlin had not stirred for at least an hour. Images flashed through his muddled brain. The marauders attacking his cabin, his brother shot down without mercy, next to him, the screams of his family as they perished in flames. Faces of men before him and the deafening roar of his avenging guns as they took the lives of those who had deprived him of everything dear to him. The scream of a woman in a lonely street. The cry of an enraged child. "Someday, I'll kill you! I hate you! I hate you!" The words drifted to silence and only the boy's tear filled face and moving lips remained fading away into the blackness of Carlin's unconsciousness.

Gradually, the blackness began to fade into gray; then light began to filter through under his eyelids. He felt a cooling sensation on his forehead and face. Water! It was spreading across his cheeks and he felt the taste of it on his swollen lips. It seemed to take tremendous effort to open his eyes, and as he willed them open to narrow slits, the brilliant light from the sun above, drove daggers of pain into his brain. He pulled the lids shut, waited a few moments, then forced them open again. This time, wider. The light was just as brilliant, but somehow, with the expectation of

THE DEVIL'S JUSTICE

it, it didn't hurt so much. His lids fluttered open and shut several times, becoming accustomed to the light. At first it was blinding and that was all he saw. Gradually, shadows began to form before him, blocking out some of the light. His eyes began to focus and he saw the shadow of a man with large hulking shoulders.

He felt giant hands beneath his own shoulders and felt his head being raised slightly off the ground. The shape of a canteen loomed into his face. He felt the coolness of water drip onto his lips and he tasted it on his tongue. With eagerness, he swallowed the liquid and thirsted for more, but it came with restraint. "Not too much at once, son," a deep resonant voice said with calm reassurance. The canteen pulled away.

Carlin's eyes began to focus on the big man's face. He saw a broad furrowed brow beneath a tattered broad brimmed hat, round glass lenses reflecting the sun's brilliant light, encircling the man's aged dark eyes, and a flowing white walrus mustache drooping off the sides of a powerful chin.

"Just take it easy boy," the voice said as the man lowered Jace's shoulders gently back onto the grass.

Carlin drifted off to unconsciousness once again. Only this time. it was a more peaceful sleep. The deep voice of his benefactor resonated in his brain. It felt soothing and somewhat familiar in a strange way. The kindly face ebbed in and out of his dreams with the same reassuring familiarity.

Then in his slumber, he found himself standing in the meadow next to the remnants of his burnt out cabin. The sky above was dark blue, filled with large, puffy, white clouds, tinged with darkness at their edges. He felt cold and empty as he stood before the three wooden crosses, staring at the final resting place of his family. He absentmindedly fingered the edge of his hat brim, that he held loosely in his hands. A cold wind tugged at his shaggy head of hair. Tears trickled down his face in icy rivulets.

"I knew you would want them buried here, Jace," a voice said from beside him.

He turned to face his long time friend, Zeke Austin. "Thanks Zeke," Carlin said.

"I knew it would be a while before you would be on your feet again after those bullets were took out of you. I figured I best take care of them myself before the townsfolk took it upon themselves to bury them in the town cemetery," Austin said.

"You figured right, old friend," Carlin put a hand on the old man's big shoulder.

Zeke Austin gave him a reassuring smile beneath his flowing white walrus mustache.

When Jace Carlin awoke again, he felt the softness of a mattress beneath him and the feather pillow beneath his head. His eyes opened and he saw the blanket tucked beneath his chin. Sunlight streamed through the window to his left. Dust particles danced in the beams.

"How're you feelin', boy?" Zeke Austin said rising from his chair and shuffled across the room toward the bed where Carlin lie. He pulled a straight chair away from the wall, dropping his heavy bulk onto the seat. His ample middle spilled over his belt and his suspenders framed the drooping belly on each side.

"I wasn't dreaming, then," Jace said . "It was you, that helped me."

"If I'd've been in your dreams, son, that must have been one wing ding of a nightmare." Zeke joked. "But, by the looks of things," he continued. "Your nightmare happened in daytime before I came along. What happened, out there, anyhow,son?"

" Two men," Jace started, his voice was raspy and it was a bit of an effort to speak. "Jumped me. Hardly saw them. They dragged me, then beat me. Did you see them?"

"No," Zeke sighed. "Not a sign of anyone out there. Just you. Not even a horse around. What were you doing on Diamond 8 land, anyhow?"

"Diamond 8?" Jace pulled himself up to a sitting position. His body ached with the movement. He glanced around the room recognizing Zeke's room as he remembered it. It was a small room that had been added to the back of Ben Crenshaw's ranch house. Zeke had been Ben's Segundo for many years. "But I heard, Ben Crenshaw sold out. You...you mean, you still work here for the new owners? I heard some bad things about them."

"Yeah, I know what you probably heard and you're wonderin' if it's true and why I'd be a part of it."

Carlin nodded.

THE DEVIL'S JUSTICE

"I'm an old man son. Ain't easy for a man like me to get work. Besides, this ranch has been my home for a long time. When Stacy Merritt asked me to stay on, I did. Can't say I agree with everything that goes on around here though."

"Guess everyone has their price, Zeke," Jace said with more than a hint of disappointment. "Still I can't see you putting up with hired guns, killing, and running people off their land."

"I don't suppose, there's much I can say about that." There was sorrow in his eyes and his voice. "But don't believe everything you hear, nuther."

"I suppose it was your men who jumped me, then," Jace said flatly. So, why did you help me?"

"You're my friend, Jace. I hope you can still believe that. But just to set the record straight, it wasn't Diamond 8 riders what done this to you. Least wise, not that I know of. Merritt doesn't admit to it. But I wouldn't put it past that hired gun, Slate."

"Morgan Slate?" Carlin said with surprise.

"You know him?"

"Heard of him. Seen him a time or two. But I wouldn't say I know him. He's mean as they come."

"That's him, alright," Austin agreed. '

"Take my advice, son. Let it go. This ain't no place for you no more. Best you ride on and forget about all this. I'll ask the boss to loan you a horse and saddle."

"Seems to me, somebody owes me a horse. But, that doesn't mean I'm leaving."

THE DEVIL'S JUSTICE

"Well, let's not tell the boss that though." Zeke agreed. "Now how about we see to you getting' some breakfast."

"Breakfast? You mean I...?"

"Yeah. You slept through the rest of yestidday and all night." The old man chuckled and started for the door. "I'll be right back with some coffee and bisquits. We can jaw some more when I get back."

The ranch looked pretty much the same as Jace Carlin had remembered it, though it did look less prosperous than it had before. Zeke and Jace strolled, leisurely, from Zeke's quarters and around the front of building, following a dirt roadway toward the barn and corrals. A man and woman were in conversation at the rails with their backs to Zeke and Jace.

"Boss!" The old man called, as they approached the corral.

The woman and the tall man next to her both turned to face the oncoming pair.

The woman was tall and looked like she could handle the ruggedness of ranch life. She was dressed in a man's red plaid shirt and jeans, rolled up atop her calfskin half boots. A gun belt encircled her lean hips and a pearl handled .38 Smith & Wesson revolver rested snugly in the holster on her right thigh and a bit to the front. Her brown range hat was tied tightly beneath a delicate chin. The crown covered the back of her head, but her curly blond hair fell free in front over her forehead and around her ears.

THE DEVIL'S JUSTICE

The tall man was dark and swarthy, with a faded dark blue shirt and jeans tucked into high top black boots. His broad face was shaved clean, but a shadow of what would have been a heavy black beard, still remained. He wore a fancy black Stetson with silver conchoes on the hat band. He had mocking black eyes that sparkled with arrogance and reflected the confidence of a dangerous man. He wore a shiny black leather Buscadero pistol rig with two holsters. Well worn black pistol grips protruded from each one. The man's fingers lightly brushed them as he moved with a catlike stealth.

They both eyed Carlin closely, sizing him up suspiciously.

"Miss Merritt, this is the young man I told you about." Zeke said when they came close. Then to Carlin, "Jace, this is Stacy Merritt."

Jace was jolted. From all he had heard about the Diamond 8's boss's ruthlessness, he had not expected that Stacy Merritt was a woman. Her face was stern and cold, but something about her blue eyes belied the fact.

"And this is……..," he started, indicating the tall man.

"Morgan Slate," Carlin filled in the rest flatly and coolly.

"And you are Jace Carlin," Slate countered. His thumbs hooked in his gunbelt and he rocked back and forth on his heels.

"I take it, you two know each other," Stacy acknowledged. There was a hardness to her voice and her face remained impassive.

THE DEVIL'S JUSTICE

"More like, we know of each other," Carlin said icily, not letting his eyes stray from Slate's face.

"Yeah," Slate drawled. "We've never met, but we know about each other. Sort of belong to the same club, so to speak. Birds of a feather, you know." He grinned slyly.

"But we don't keep to the same flock," Carlin added.

"Pretend what you want, Carlin. But we both know we're the same kind of bird."

Jace's face reddened and his jaw tightened. Anger flashed in his eyes.

"That's enough preening your feathers for now, boys," Stacy put in harshly. "Both of you, back off before I cool your tail feathers, myself."

"Now, I just might enjoy that," Morgan chuckled. He cut it short when he recognized the fire growing in Stacy Merritt's glare. He backed off.

"I've heard about you too, Mister Carlin," Stacy said, addressing her attention to Carlin, "From what I've heard, Morgan is right, but Zeke told me I shouldn't believe everything I hear."

"That's funny," Jace answered. "That's what Zeke told me about you." He stared coldly into her eyes for a moment, letting the meaning set in.

Breaking the tension, Zeke put in, "I told Jace, he could borrow a horse. Is that all right, Miss Merritt?"

"Sure," she answered. "He can keep the horse. That way he's got no reason to come back."

Zeke was taken back. "Well boss, that's no way to...."

THE DEVIL'S JUSTICE

"You may think he's your friend, Zeke. And that's the only reason I wouldn't have Slate shoot him right now."

Slate smirked, victoriously.

Then to Carlin, Stacy warned, "Take what ever horse you want and a saddle. Then get off the Diamond 8 and don't come back."

She turned and walked away, crooking a finger in the air for slate. "Morgan," she summoned without slowing her step. The gunman grinned, tipped his hat brim mockingly to Carlin and followed after her.

It was almost noon when Jace Carlin pulled rein in front of the Sheriff's office in Contention Springs. He dismounted the rangy grulla, he had taken from the Diamond 8, and tied up at the hitch rail.

Will Parmalee was sitting at a wooden desk, when Jace came through the doorway. He looked up and his eyes roamed over Jace's bruised face, torn shirt and dirty jeans. "What happened to you?" He asked dryly without feigning a hint of surprise nor concern.

"Two men jumped me out at my place. There's Diamond 8 cattle there, grazing on my grass."

"And?"

"And I want to know what you're going to do about it."

Parmalee sighed, rose from his chair and moved to the front of his desk and sat on a corner. "There's nothing I can do about it," he said. "You were trespassing."

THE DEVIL'S JUSTICE

"Trespassing?" Carlin charged at him, his face flushed and anger in his eyes. "I was on my own property!"

Parmalee shook his head from side to side. "No, you weren't. That land doesn't belong to you any more."

"Doesn't belong to me? What are you talking about? We built that spread up out of a wilderness. My brother and I. We put our lives into it. Our sweat and blood."

"I know. I know, Jace," the Sheriff said quietly, trying to calm him down. "But you've been gone for four years. The taxes weren't being paid and for all intents and purposes, that land was regarded as abandoned. The county had no choice but to sell it for back taxes."

"Then I'll pay the damn taxes. I want my home back."

"I'm afraid it's too late for that, Jace. Just way too late. I told you it would've been best for you to just ride on. Start fresh somewhere else."

"I don't want somewhere else. My family is buried there," His eyes bulged with anger. "That's another thing," he ranted. "They've taken away the grave markers and let the grass grow up. I can't even find where my family lies and cattle are tramping over them; grazing."

"I'm sorry, Jace. There's nothing I can do. What did you expect."

"Justice!" Carlin growled.

"This is justice, Jace. The property no longer belongs to you. It's the law."

"The law?" Jace hissed. "The law did nothing when my family was taken from me and now it's doing nothing when my land is being taken."

"You gave your land up, Jace. To go on a vengeance quest, searching for the justice you thought was owed you. But did you get justice? No. Only vengeance. Only the law can collect justice."

"That's why I came here, Will," Jace's tact began to soften. "I thought I'd give the law another chance to do it right, but I see I was wrong." He turned on his heel and left.

Will Parmalee watched him go. The furrows of his brow deepened and he felt a chill along his spine.

Carlin was still angry an hour later when he emerged from the hotel. After leaving the sheriff's office, Jace had returned to his room and washed up again, changed into clean clothes and rested on the bed for a while, just thinking and remembering.. His home was gone and the law was not going to help. Did he have to take matters into his own hands again? "No!" he told himself. He had sought vengeance before and found it empty. He hoped he had learned something, but to return to a vengeance trail, would mean that he had learned nothing. Perhaps, he should take everyone's advice and move on. No! He couldn't do that either. He couldn't let his own land be taken from him. He could not allow his family to lie in unmarked, forgotten graves, with cattle tramping over them.

He jumped up from the bed and grasped his saddle bags from the back of a straight chair. He

THE DEVIL'S JUSTICE

hefted it, feeling the weight of its contents. He jerked open the flap and pulled the coiled pistol belt and Colt.45 from it. With practiced ease, he slid the weapon from the well oiled holster. He held it firmly in his hand, feeling the smooth handle and savoring how it felt in his palm, as he hefted it's balance. He worked the hammer and mechanism and checked the loads. A familiar rush waved over him.

Then he held himself in check, for a moment. What was he doing? Was he still a slave to this awesome power in his hand?

No!

He slammed the Colt back into its sheath and tossed the gun belt onto the bed, donned his range hat, opened the door and went out, leaving the gun behind.

And now as he stepped off the hotel porch steps, he heard a familiar female voice from down the street. "Jace! Jace Carlin! It really is you."

As he turned on his heel, he heard the rustle of skirts and out of the corner of his eye, for a fleeting moment, he thought he saw his own beloved Alice, rushing toward him. But that was impossible, she was dead and gone. Never to return to him. As realization set in, he saw it was Alice's sister Jenna. She and Alice had always looked so much alike. He hardly had time to compose himself, when she was already upon him; dropping her packages and throwing her arms around Jace's neck and squealing with delight.

"Oh Jace. You've come back. It's so good to see you again."

THE DEVIL'S JUSTICE

At first, Carlin was numb by the surprise and the sudden rush of affection. He stood woodenly as she hugged and kissed him. Then as if a switch had been turned on, he responded. He wrapped his arms around her tightly and buried his face in her hair, his cheek against hers and remembered the familiar perfume, from times gone by when he and Jenna had been an item before Jace had turned his attentions to Alice. He hugged her tightly. Then as her excitedness subsided, they mutually released each other, stood back and smiled to one another. For a brief moment, neither had a word to say. Then they both started at once. They laughed.

"You first," Jace said sheepishly.

"Oh, no, Jace Carlin. I already got in the first words."

Jace shifted uneasily on his feet. He felt awkward. "'Good to see you again, Jenna," he said. "You...you look good."

"I wish I could say the same for you," she said, letting her dark eyes roam over Jace Carlin's bruised face. "What happened to you. You look like you got caught in a buzz saw."

"Jace forced a chuckle and made light of it. "Just a little accident," he said noncommittally. "It's nothing. Really."

"Doesn't look like nothing to me." Then she dropped the matter. "My, my, Jace Carlin," she repeated as if admiring him. She gazed into his eyes and he glanced nervously away. "Just wait until Duncan sees you. He'll be so happy. He's missed you these many years. He always regarded you as his best friend."

THE DEVIL'S JUSTICE

That was true. Duncan and Jace had been the best of friends for years. When Jace married Alice, Duncan Holt had been his best man. Then when Duncan married Jenna, Jace was the best man. Jace had recovered from his gunshot wounds at Duncan's ranch, but Duncan had not been successful in dissuading Jace from riding the vengeance trail.

"I'm just finishing my shopping, Jace. How about coming out to the ranch with me? Have supper with us."

"I... really shouldn't," he protested meekly.

"Nonsense," Jenna insisted. "Duncan would be so disappointed. You can't let him down. Now, can you?"

"It's just...just that I have some matters to attend to." He didn't know what else to say.

"Can't it wait?" Jenna pleaded.

"Well..."

"I'm not taking no for an answer, Jace Carlin. Whatever you've got to do, can just wait. Besides, I'm in town all by myself and I could use a big strong man to drive me back in my buggy. You know I never was much good at handling horses." She took him by the arm and pulled. "Now are you coming with me or do I have to drag you all the way home?"

Jace grinned. "Looks like I don't have a choice, do I?"

"No you don't," she said emphatically with a giggle.

"I guess we ought to pick up these packages, then. Can't leave them lying in the street," Jace said, stooping to gather them up.

THE DEVIL'S JUSTICE

They were still laughing as they walked down the street to where the buggy was parked. Jace loaded the packages and helped Jenna into the rig. Then he climbed aboard, took the reins, clucked to the sleek black gelding in the traces, and made a u turn in the street. He stopped briefly across from the hotel to retrieve the grulla and tie him on behind the carriage.

As he tooled the carriage along the street, he was well aware of people staring and watching him. He tried not to turn his head in either direction, to show that he was aware, but out of the corner of his eye he noticed Amy Parker in the open doorway of the Clarion, watching with interest.

As they past by the sheriff's office, reflected light off the window panes precluded him from seeing Will Parmalee, but the back of his neck bristled and somehow , he knew Parmalee was also watching.

Carlin tried to concentrate on his driving. He slapped the reins at the black and hurried his step as they rode on out of town.

The drive was pleasant and Jace found himself becoming less uncomfortable. Jenna provided most of the conversation, most of it small talk and catching him up on some of the local news and gossip and reminiscing about old times. Conspicuously absent from the conversation was any mention about trouble in the valley and Jace chose not to ask.

Duncan Holt's ranch was a mere half hour ride from town and as the buggy rolled through the main gate of the Rafter H. Jace noted that the ranch had changed somewhat. The ranch house had been expanded outwards and upwards and was now a two story structure with a fresh coat of white paint. The grounds had been expertly landscaped and exuded an air of elegance. Duncan Holt had prospered substantially while Jace had been away.

A new barn, bunkhouse, and additional outbuildings had been built as well as expanding the main corral and adding two smaller ones. And in one of them, he saw a familiar looking gray mare. His mare.

His eyes were still fixed on the mare, with disbelief as he passed the gates and had swung the buggy onto the curve of the driveway, leading toward the house when he saw two men emerge from the barn and head toward the main corral. He only caught a glimpse of them as they turned away from him, but he recognized them immediately. Their images had been burnt indelibly into his brain. One had a flaming red beard and the other, a man with a black stubbled beard.

THE DEVIL'S JUSTICE

Chapter Four

Instinctively, Jace Carlin whipped the horse into a run. The carriage jolted forward with a lunge. Jenna, taken by surprise, let out a short scream and shot a hand to the back of her head, holding her bonnet in place.

Carlin drove the horse off the driveway into the barnyard; the carriage wheels slewing sideways, churning up dust and debris. The two men were turning in surprise as the horse and carriage almost slid into them. Carlin pulled the horse up short, forcing him to slide to a stop, almost on his haunches. In the same instant, he tossed the reins into Jenna's lap, and without making sure that she was in control of the leathers, he leaped from the seat, diving in mid air between the two men. He hit them hard, each arm and shoulder taking each of them down.

He had surprise on his side and was able to recover first. While the two stunned men rolled in the dirt, he jumped to his feet with catlike quickness. As he did so, his fingers reached inside red beard's collar and pulled the man to his feet with him.

Still holding red beard upright with his left, he released his right and smashed a round house blow into his face. The sound of bone cracking

THE DEVIL'S JUSTICE

was followed by a gush of bright red blood spewing from red beard's mashed bulbous nose.

Carlin released him, letting him fall into his partner, who was trying to get up behind red beard. The two fell to the ground, their bodies intertwined in confused flailing. Carlin came after them, keeping his momentum and element of surprise. His face was cold as chiseled stone and his eyes were blank and devoid of feeling. He pulled the man with the black stubble to his feet. He held him in place and sunk his right fist into the man's belly, without giving him room to double up or fall. He swung his fist into the man's face. It whipped to the side with a crack. Blood, sprayed out from between his teeth. Then, once again, Carlin buried his fist in the man's midsection. This time he stepped aside and let him fall to the ground on top of the writhing red beard.

Meanwhile, Jenna Holt had taken control of the reins and brought the startled horse to a halt. She was climbing down from the carriage seat, when the door to the ranch house burst open and a tall man of about thirty, with huge shoulders and broad back, well groomed blond hair and a bristly blond mustache ran out into the ranch yard. He wore a white shirt, with the shirt sleeves rolled halfway up his forearms and his black string tie hung loose beneath his collar, as if he had been relaxing. He first ran to Jenna, making sure she was all right; then ran behind Jace Carlin.

His strong arms wrapped around Jace's shoulders, pinning his arms to his side. He lifted Carlin off the ground, letting his toes dangle. Carlin tried to squirm free, but could only swing his legs. The big man, rocked back and forth on his feet, swinging Jace from side to side, increasing the arc swing and building momentum. Then he let him go and Jace went flying headlong across the yard. He landed, hard, on his right shoulder. It was still hurting from the beating he had taken the day before and now it hurt even more.

Instinctively, he rolled to the side and pushed himself to his feet in a crouch. His right hand automatically went to his thigh, reaching for the gun that wasn't there. He froze in place when he realized that he was unarmed and as the haze drifted away from his enraged eyes and he began to focus, he finally saw the big man before him clearly, for the first time.

"Jace! Jace Carlin!" The big man exclaimed, recognizing his old friend. He came forward quickly, extending a big hand in friendship. "You old son of a gun," he said. "When did you get back?"

It seemed as if he had forgotten about the two beaten men, on the ground as he stepped forward, until he heard red beard groan as he was rolling over and sitting up in the dirt, his hand covering his bloody nose. The other man was stirring also.

"Hello, Duncan," Jace said through his labored breathing, without moving from his crouched stance and not reaching for the offered hand.

Duncan Holt rubbed his thumb and forefinger together as if in disdain and pulled his hand away. "I guess the better question," he said. "is what the hell is going on here?"

"I'm the one who should be asking questions," Jace snarled. "What the hell are you doing with my horse in your corral?" He arched his neck, pointing his chin toward the corral. "And why did you have your men beat up on me yesterday."

"Wh...what are you talking about?" Duncan Holt asked unbelievingly.

"These two men jumped me on my spread yesterday. Beat the tar out of me and stole my horse. It's the gray mare in your corral."

Holt glanced over his shoulder and saw the horse. Then to his two men who were now struggling to get to their feet. "Is that right, Lacy?"

Red Lacy was sitting up now, rubbing his red bearded chin. "Yeah. That's him. I told you about it yesterday."

"You didn't tell me he was a friend of mine." Holt bellowed.

"How was we supposed to know, boss?" Red said chagrined. "You said to keep everyone off your property."

"Your property?" Carlin exclaimed, his eyes round and wide open. "But the cattle were branded Diamond 8." Then he added. "Wait a minute. Just how did you get my spread, anyhow?"

Duncan rubbed a finger behind his ear and said, "Well, now. I guess I have some explaining to do, at that. Come on in the house and we'll talk about it." He motioned to the front door, turned on his heel and headed for it, ignoring his beaten two men. Jenna was waiting at the door, consternation on her face.

Jace stood slowly, watching him go and trying to make sense of it all. His face was still flushed with anger. He clenched his jaw and followed after Holt.

"This ain't over, cowboy," Red Lacy called to him from behind.

Jace Carlin halted a moment, turned slowly; his eyes glaring at the two men who had now risen to their feet and were dusting themselves off. "That's right," he said flatly. "It ain't over."

He turned and stepped up onto the porch and allowed Duncan Holt to usher him through the doorway.

"So you see, Jace," Duncan said. "It was all a mistake. I really am sorry about it." He was standing beside his red brick fireplace, leaning against the mantle and poking tobacco into his pipe.

"So am I," Jace said soberly. He tried to force a half smile. He was sitting in one of the plush upholstered chairs in the living room. The place had really changed since the last time, Jace had been there. The highly polished floors were mostly covered with expensive carpets and the furniture was very elegant and luxurious. Jace felt uneasy, placing the seat of his dusty jeans on such an expensive chair. He sat forward of the cushion leaned over his knees, nervously fingering his range hat in his hands.

"I'll make sure, it doesn't happen again. I'll introduce you to my men, so there will be no mistake, next time. You've already met Red Lacy and Burl Riley."

"Yes. And I don't think they'll forget it too soon."

"I'll talk to them. They won't give you any more trouble. I promise you that."

Jace nodded, but to himself, he thought he better not let his guard down, concerning those two. Then he said, "So, how is it you're calling my place yours,"

"Well Jace," Holt said, striking a match and dipping it above the bowl of his pipe. He puffed at the stem, until the smoke trickled upward. "You'd been gone a long time. We'd all read about you in the papers and everyone assumed you'd never come back." He said around the stem of the pipe, through clenched teeth.

"Well, they assumed wrong," Carlin said with an edge of bitterness.

Holt withdrew the pipe, blew out a puff of smoke and smiled. "As we can see now." Then he continued, "The place was growing up to weeds and the stock had drifted off. The taxes hadn't been paid for years, so the county auctioned it off. I couldn't let the Diamond 8 get their hands on it. Lord knows they've already driven away many of the smaller ranchers, many of them your friends; and gobbled up their lands."

Jace remained silent, listening.

"So, I outbid them and took it myself. Paid a lot more than what it was worth."

"It's good land. Worth a lot," Carlin interjected in protest.

THE DEVIL'S JUSTICE

"To you, yes," Duncan agreed. "To me, I only wanted to keep the Diamond 8 out."

"Why did you take my family's grave markers down?"

Duncan stammered and shifted side to side on his feet. "I...I didn't know your family was buried there. I assumed they were buried in the town cemetery."

"Seems to me, there's been a lot of assuming going on around here," Jace said icily.

"I'm sorry, Jace," Duncan's brow furrowed in a frown. "My men must have cleared the markers away when they cleared the land of what was left of the buildings. It was a mistake, I'm sure. I never would have let that happen had I known about it. You and I can ride out there and see if we can relocate the graves and remark them."

"No," Jace growled bitterly. "I'll do it myself. I want my land back."

"Of course you do," Holt retorted. "And, I'll sell it back to you for what I paid for it."

Jace flustered and twisted a chagrined smile. "You will? You really mean that, Duncan?" He came up out of his chair, offering him his hand.. You always were my best friend. I shouldn't have doubted you. I'm awfully sorry about my attitude I came in here with."

Duncan took his hand and gripped it tight. He said without letting go. "Never forget, I'm your friend, good buddy. But, before you get too carried away, I'd better tell you what it'll cost you." He released his grip and pulled his hand away.

THE DEVIL'S JUSTICE

The excitement died in Jace's eyes. "Can't be that much," he said weakly; apprehension building in his voice. He stared into Holt's eyes expectantly.

Duncan held his stare for a moment, then blurted it out. "It's six thousand dollars, Jace." There was a hint of sadness in his eyes.

Carlin's jaw dropped. He was stunned. "Six thousand? I...I don't understand." His head bowed and his words were mumbled. Then as realization sunk in, his head jerked upward, his face turning red with anger once again. "What are you trying to pull? You know it's not worth any where near that."

Holt arched his back away, throwing up both hands, palms flat forward as if warding off an attack. "Just hold on there, Jace. Just hear me out."

Jace backed off, restraining himself and glaring.

"We both know that it's not worth that much. But that's what I had to pay to keep the Diamond 8 from getting it."

"That was one hell of a price," Carlin said.

"You're telling me," Duncan agreed. "But if they had gotten your spread, they would never sell it back to you. I will. That's the good part. I really don't need the land. I'd rather have you back on it and be my neighbor again."

"I haven't got six thousand dollars," Jace said dejectedly. "Might as well be six million. Hell, I haven't even got six hundred." Then a thought occurred to him. "Maybe you could let me work it off. Pay it over time."

THE DEVIL'S JUSTICE

Holt shook his head. "Wish I could Jace, but I've got a mortgage on it. I know it must look to you that I'm doing well, but between the trouble the Diamond 8 has been giving me and all the rustling going on, I've stretched myself financially."

"Rustling?"

"Yeah. And it's my guess that the Diamond 8 is behind that too. You said you saw Diamond 8 cattle on your spread. My guess is they were Rafter H cows that had been rustled and had their brands run over and then had wandered back onto your spread looking for their calves."

Jace pondered a moment, then said, "You sure it isn't the other way around? I mean, your men didn't accidentally haze in some Diamond 8 stock by mistake."

"You know me better than that, Jace. I'm no rustler."

"No. But I'm not so sure about those two idiots you have working for you."

"Lacy and Riley? No. They may be stupid, but I don't think they're that stupid. They know what I'd do to them, if I caught them."

"Just what would you do to them?" Jace asked coolly.

Duncan grinned. "I dunno," he shook his head. "Just spouting off I suppose. But tell you what. We'll go out there and skin one of those critters and I'll bet you dollars to donuts that the other side of the hide will show where a Rafter H was changed into a Diamond 8."

THE DEVIL'S JUSTICE

"Well, I guess that would have been easy enough to do. Your brand is a natural to change into theirs."

"Sure it is," Duncan said. "I'm sure that's why they chose the brand they did"

"Can't you do something about it?" Carlin queried. "What about Parmalee? He's the sheriff now. Can't he do something about it.?"

"If we had proof, yes. But so far we haven't caught them with the goods. Parmalee is a good man, but without proof, his hands are tied."

"Amy Parker told me that the Diamond 8 bunch killed Randy Poole. What about that?"

"Again, no proof, even though everybody knows Morgan Slate did it.. He's the hired gunman that Stacy Merrit hired to do her dirty work. He's a mean one. No one wants to brace him. Not even Parmalee."

"I know him," Jace responded flatly. "I wouldn't underestimate him, but I think he's more bully and braggart, than expert gunman. Don't get me wrong. He'll shoot you in the back or from ambush if he can. He'll just never give anyone an even break. He's just not that fast."

"Think you could take him?" Holt asked, his interest rising.

"Maybe, if I played by his rules and didn't give him an even break either." Then he paused with realization. "Say. Just what are you getting at, Duncan?"

"We've heard a lot about you, while you were away. You've built yourself quite a reputation. They say you're fast. A real Coltman. Maybe you could help us out."

THE DEVIL'S JUSTICE

"Oh, no," Jace said shaking his head back and forth. "I'm through with guns and fighting. I've had enough."

"I noticed you weren't wearing a gun," Holt said. "Are you sure that's wise?"

"Why not? My home is here. All I want is to get my spread back and to be left alone."

"But that won't happen as long as there is trouble in the valley. As long as the Diamond 8 keeps pushing us and grabbing up the range, none of us are going to keep our homes. If you're going to stay here, you'd better be ready to fight."

Jace lowered his head and stared at the plush carpet. "Otherwise," Holt continued. "You'd better ride on."

Jace jerked his head upward and his dark eyes flashed with anger. "Nobody's chasing me away."

"Then help us Jace. You're the only one around here, who can stand up to Slate. Put that gun on one more time. Rid us of this monster and the Diamond 8 will have to back off."

"Merritt will just bring in another gunman," Jace said.

"I don't think so. As long as you are here, she'll have a tough time getting anyone else to buy in."

Carlin remained silent. Duncan continued. "You want your land back. You haven't got $6000 to buy it back. But what if I can get the other ranchers to go along with it, maybe you can earn it."

"I'm not a hired gun," Carlin growled indignantly.

74

THE DEVIL'S JUSTICE

"Of course not, Jace," Holt replied. "I didn't mean it that way. But if we can work together on this, maybe we can all keep what's ours and you can get own spread back."

Jace remained silent; glaring, but not seeing Duncan Holt in front of him. His eyes pulled together in thought, fighting the urge to see it Duncan's way.

"Come on, Jace," Holt urged. "You know this is the only way."

Chapter Five

The walnut grips of the .44 Colt were well worn and smooth from constant use. The varnish had worn almost completely off and the light brown grain had a shine to it. The bright summer sun glinted off the gunmetal blue of the exposed trigger guard and cylinder and the end of the gun barrel that protruded from the plain brown leather holster. By itself, the gun in its holster was like a piece of artwork; its fine crafted lines blending into a sight to behold, neither good nor bad in itself, but riding high on a gunman's hip tied down against his thigh, the piece turned into a tool of threatening menace.

Jace Carlin rode tall in the saddle. He rode with practiced ease feeling the familiar reassuring weight of the weapon against his leg. He hated to admit it to himself, so he didn't, that it was like an old friend that had returned and had given him comfort. There was the familiar rush of adrenaline flowing through his veins and the thrill of the hunt had returned, but he tried to tell himself that he hated it, knowing that he was riding with a purpose once again.

It was still early morning after his visit with Duncan Holt the day before, when he crossed over onto Diamond 8 range. He was once again riding his own gray mare and leading the Diamond 8 horse that Stacy Merritt had lent him. Actually, she had given it to him to keep him from returning, but Carlin was returning the horse anyways. It was a good excuse to come back. He had been wary for the past several minutes as he rode on, expecting trouble at any moment and hoping to carry out his plan without gunplay.

He rode along a dry wash and emerged into large rolling grasslands that extended for miles. Cattle grazed, lazily, almost as far as the eye could see. There were no punchers insight to nursemaid them. This was strictly grazing range and the herd roamed free. He rode into the herd, guiding his mount and led horse among them where he wouldn't be as noticeable.

The herd was of fine stock. Shorthorn Herefords mostly and they were well fed. A herd like this would survive a drive up north with enough fat left on them to demand a good price for beef. His legs brushed against their hides as he meandered across the meadows. The cattle paid little attention to the rider and only moved slightly to let the man and his horses through.

Carlin noted that a good share of the herd still carried Ben Crenshaw's brand, the Slash C. The rest carried the new Diamond 8 brand. It would be easy enough to change the old Slash C into the Diamond 8 brand, but either Stacy Merritt had not wanted to nor had the time to make the conversion. He noted however, that there were no Rafter H brands among them. Of course, some of these Diamond 8 brands could have been placed over Holt's brand. He ran his hand along the hide of a steer here and there, examining the brand. Although the brands were fresh, they didn't appear to have been altered. But, without skinning off the hide and examining the underside, it was difficult to tell for sure.

Half an hour later, Carlin had left the herd and grazing range far behind. So far, so good. No trouble. He had not even seen a rider, but now he could see smoke above the trees ahead, probably from a chimney in the distance. He knew the main ranch house was in the next valley beyond a stand of cottonwoods and soon he would see signs of life.

It was as he emerged from the cottonwoods, that the rifle fire started. With the first blast, his range hat flew off his head and hung from his loose chin strap down his back. He immediately pulled the mare up sharply, to a halt as rifle slugs drilled into the sod just in front of the horse's front hoofs. He lifted his hands high, still holding the reins, and offering no resistance.

Three riders came up from the right. One circled around to his left and grasped the mare's bridle. There was a pistol in his other hand.

The other two riders were Stacy Merritt and Morgan Slate. They pulled to a halt in front of Carlin. Stacy's face was red with fire and she held a rifle, one handed, barrel pointing directly at Carlin's chest. Slate had an amused look on his face. His guns were still in their holsters and he shifted his weight in the saddle.

"I told you to stay off Diamond 8 range, Mister." The rifle barrel came close under Carlin's chin and he arched his neck backwards.

THE DEVIL'S JUSTICE

"Just bringing your horse back, ma'am," Jace said calmly, his eyes seeming to cross as he eyed the gun barrel warily.

"I told you, I didn't want the damn horse back."

"You want I should take him out now, boss?" Morgan Slate chided, a gleam in his eye.

Jace ignored him, kept his attention on Stacy. "But, I couldn't take charity, like that. Besides, I got my own horse back and found out I was mistaken about a few things."

"Well, you're still mistaken, Mister. It was a big mistake coming back here. It just might be your last," the girl said.

"If you'll just point that cannon away from my face for a minute, maybe I can tell you that I found out you had nothing to do with what happened to me the other day. I know now that you didn't steal my land."

"Of course, I didn't steal your land. Duncan Holt did."

He found it hard to hear the words, even though he knew better. "I know that now," Carlin said. "It was his men that beat up on me and took my horse. Lacy and Riley. Know them?"

"Yeah, I know them. Low life scum."

"Gave them a beating, they won't forget," Carlin said. "I'm going to have to look out for them. Wouldn't put it past them to try to drygulch me."

"That would be just too bad," Slate said. "I'm hoping to get my chance at you first."

"Dry gulching is your style, isn't it Slate?"

"I could take you down in a standup fight, anytime, Carlin. And you know it," Slate scoffed.

"Enough of that, Morgan," Stacy warned, not taking her eyes off Carlin. Slate let his mount step back.

"I need to get back at Holt," Jace said, ignoring the whole tirade. "I was hoping we could team up."

"Why would I want to team up with you?" She answered.

"Some say I'm good with a gun."

Slate just shrugged at that.

"I know you're good with a gun, but I don't hire guns."

Jace glanced at Morgan Slate. "Oh, no. What about him?"

"I'm her partner," Slate interjected, mockingly. "And I don't hire guns either."

"Not yet," Stacy snapped."you're not a partner until I say so.".

Carlin was a bit taken back by these remarks. He wondered just what it all meant, but he dared not let on. "Well maybe you don't think you need my help, but I need yours. Seems to me, we both want to get back at Duncan Holt and I want my land back. A temporary alliance might be beneficial to both of us. Holt thinks I bought his lies about you and thinks I'm still his friend. Being on the inside working him from the middle while you blindside him might be the way to take him down."

Stacy's eyes softened a bit. Jace could tell that she was starting to think on it. "Sure, you got Slate to back you up. But, why not have both of us? I can work with Slate." He glanced toward the gunman. "Unless, he's too arrogant to work with me."

"I'll show you how arrogant I am. With the hot end of a pistol." Slate retorted, his right hand drifting toward the butt of his pistol.

"Morgan!" Stacy snapped sharply. "How many times do I have to tell you to back off."

Slate grimaced and brought his hand back to the reins.

"Maybe, Carlin's right. Maybe we should join forces," Stacy said. She lowered the rifle and Jace breathed a sigh of relief as he relaxed in the saddle and lowered his arms..

"I still think you're mistaken," Slate grumbled, glowering at Carlin, edging his horse back a little further as if he were too close to a rattlesnake.

"Must I remind you, Morgan," Stacy said. "I still do the thinking around here."

Slate pursed his lips with chagrin and looked away momentarily. Then to Carlin, he said, "Alright, for now, we work together, but when this is all over and we have no further need of each other, then we settle things between us."

"I'm sure we will," Jace said icily. Then he reached behind his back and slid his hat around front. He poked his finger through the bullet hole in the crown and said playfully to Stacy, "I just bought this hat new. I'm getting tired of replacing hats."

"I'll buy you a damned hat when you've earned it," she said with annoyance.

THE DEVIL'S JUSTICE

He smiled, put the hat back on his head and tightened the chin strap. "Fair enough," he said.

"Now, as I told you yesterday," Jace said. "I assumed you had taken over my spread because I saw grazing cattle wearing the Diamond 8 brand. I would think you'd want them back as proof that Holt rustled your cattle. You could go to Parmalee and have Holt arrested."

"Parmalee?" Stacy scoffed. "He's in Duncan Holt's pocket. The only law we got here is our own guns."

"Then why don't we use them?" Carlin urged. "Let's go get them back. If Holt tries to stop us, we fight."

"Range war, you mean," Stacy answered.

"Seems to me you already have it. It's just been simmering. Maybe it's time to bring it to a boil."

"I guess it is," Stacy said with a bit of regret, but rich with resolve. "Then, let's go get them."

Morgan Slate grinned broadly. He was going to use his gun..

They were twelve riders strong when they galloped into the basin where Jace Carlin had once called home. Cattle were grazing contentedly in the lush meadows. There was no sight of Rafter H riders about. As they rode onto the range, Carlin hauled back sharply on the reins and lifted his hand skyward in signal to Stacy, Slate and the other nine riders, urging them to slow the pace. To ride pell mell into the herd would mean startling the cattle and sending them into a milling swirl of confusion.

THE DEVIL'S JUSTICE

They rode slowly into the herd, each rider spreading out away from the others, loosening their lariats from the saddles and seeking out the cattle with Diamond 8 brands. They shook out their loops and began cutting the animals out and herding them into a smaller herd away from the main bunch. They worked the better part of two hours. By mid afternoon they had culled most, if not all of them, out of the bunch. They were no longer readily finding Diamond 8 brands among the primary herd and Stacy was satisfied with what they had..

"Alright, boys!" Stacy Merritt shouted riding toward the head of her herd. "Let's take them home."

The riders took up positions on flanks, swings, and drag. Stacy, Slate and Carlin took point. Morgan Slate seemed a little glum; disappointed that there had been no confrontation with Holt's riders.

"Cheer up, Morgan," Jace chided. "We're not home yet. You may get your chance at trouble yet."

"Something about this seems fishy to me," Slate growled. "Too damned easy if you ask me."

"Nobody's asking you, Morgan," Stacy put in. "Don't be in such a hurry for trouble. When Holt finds out we took our cattle back, we'll have our full share of trouble sooner than we may want."

"Well, it can't come soon enough to suit me," Slate boasted.

"That's good, Morgan," Jace drawled. "'Cause here it comes, now." He reined his horse to a halt, signaling the other riders to contain the herd.

Two large groups of riders, guns in hands, came over the ridges on each side of the basin and were barreling down on top of them. The riders from the right were led by Duncan Holt himself while the riders on the left were led by Will Parmalee. The late afternoon sun glinted off the five pointed star on his vest.

The sudden appearance of riders frightened the steers and they began to scatter, brushing against the Diamond 8 punchers' horses and pushing them off balance. At the same time the lead steers pushed forward, forcing Carlin, Slate, and Merritt to separate, allowing the cattle to pass through ahead of them.

Slate sidled his mount sideways, moving out of their way and turned to face the riders from the left. His face went pale, then he forced a bravado smile and pulled both pistols from their holsters. He seemed to fumble with them as he tried to hang onto the reins and control his skittering mount.

"Hold it!" Carlin shouted, jumping his mare forward and grasping Slate's left gun arm. "There's too many of them. And were caught in the middle of the herd."

"What the hell are you doing?" Slate swore and shook him off, sidling his horse away and raising his guns. Both pistols belched and flame spat from the muzzles. Through the fog of clouding gunsmoke, Slate saw one of Parmalee's riders pitch backward from his saddle and fell wounded into the grass. The oncoming riders slowed their pace, sidestepping their horses around

THE DEVIL'S JUSTICE

the man as he scurried out of the way of oncoming hooves. The posse opened return fire at Slate.

Bullets whined over Morgan Slate's head and one chewed a chunk out the front right side of his hat brim. Carlin charged his mare, once again, at Slates's steed, and slammed solidly into the animal's side, pushing Slate out the way as another slug buzzed past his ear. The impact upset Slate in the saddle. His rear raised out of the saddle, but he remained standing in the stirrups. The sudden jolt forced him to drop his guns and he grasped the pommel of his saddle to retain his perch.

Carlin leaped from his own saddle, slamming into Morgan Slate, wrapping his arms around the gunman's large frame, lifting him completely out of the saddle and landing on top of him as they fell heavily, beneath their horses' feet and rolled in the tall grass while frightened cattle rushed by, barely missing them. As much as Jace hated the man, he hovered over Slate's body, holding him down and protecting him from the sharp hooves.

As the onslaught of passing cattle subsided, Jace eased up the pressure on the gunman. Morgan Slate twisted beneath Carlin, pulled his right arm free, cocking it and slamming his fist upward, driving a solid blow under Jace's chin. Stunned by the blow, Jace fell backward and landed flat on his back in the grass. Slated vaulted halfway to his feet, stretching his body and diving forward, landing across Jace's form and wrapping his huge hands around Carlin's throat, digging his knuckles deep into the flesh.

THE DEVIL'S JUSTICE

Jace gasped for breath, but Slate squeezed tighter. Carlin felt lightheaded and blackness started to cloud his brain. He was about to pass out when he felt the pressure release. He suddenly tasted a breath of air and he tried to suck it in. At first, it seemed like all he could draw in was more pain. His throat felt tight and ached as if it had a large ball lodged inside. Then the muscles seemed to relax and he felt the first full breath of air. It felt cool and overwhelming. His lungs filled and contracted. Then another breath, and another until he was breathing fully once again. His throat still ached, but the pain was beginning to subside. His brain started to clear. The darkness dissolved into light and soon his vision started to return. At first it was just light, then patches of color, gradually melting into shapes. Slowly, the shapes came into focus and he could see plainly now. He sat up in the grass, rubbing his neck, and looking round.

Parmalee and two of his posse had Morgan Slate on his feet and held in restraint. Slate struggled violently within their grasp, but it was to no avail. He glared with anger, swore vehemently, and tried to spit in Parmalee's face. But the lawman merely leaned back out of spitting range and chuckled at his prisoner's plight.

The herd had scattered and was still running. Possemen and Holt riders held the Diamond 8 punchers at bay. Stacy Merritt sat calmly in her saddle, accepting their capture. "Morgan!" She shouted. "Give it up. There's nothing we can do right now."

"Listen to your boss, Slate," Parmalee urged. "It'll all go easier, if you don't fight it."

THE DEVIL'S JUSTICE

"Go to hell," Slate growled.

"Morgan!" Stacy repeated. "Do as I say."

Slate jerked his head toward Stacy Merritt. He saw riders with guns out, sitting their horses in a semi circle around her. He glanced around, saw other riders holding guns on the other punchers. He saw Carlin pushing himself to his feet. The sight of Carlin drove his anger to a new level and he blurted a stream of obscenities at him.

"That's enough, Morgan," Stacy ordered. She glowered at him with determination. He stopped struggling against his captors, feeling relief from the struggle, and stared back at her in astonishment. "But, it's all his fault, Stace. You know that. He lured us up here into a trap."

"Yes, I know," she said contemptuously. She glared at Jace as he came to his feet and adjusted his hat. To Jace she said, "I suppose you think you're pretty clever, Mister Carlin. But, you're just plain stupid. You chose the wrong side. Now you'll never get your land back." She looked away, not wanting to see him anymore.

Carlin glanced toward Duncan Holt, who was still on his horse and observing the situation with the air of a supervisor. Duncan, half smiled reassuringly to Jace, that he had, indeed, done the right thing. Jace felt a chill and a pang of regret. He quickly dismissed the fleeting hint of distrust that momentarily came over him, when Duncan nodded to Parmalee.

"Get Slate on his horse, men," Parmalee ordered his posse. Then to Jace, "Unbuckle your gunbelt and get on your horse."

Then to Stacy, he said, "You're all under arrest for cattle rustling."

"You're arresting the wrong people, Sheriff," Stacy Merritt responded. "Duncan Holt stole these steers from me. We were merely taking them back. You'll notice they all have a Diamond 8 brand."

"I think if you'll look close, Sheriff," Holt said. "You'll find those brands have been changed from a Rafter H to a Diamond 8."

"That's a lie," Stacy said. "See for yourself."

Parmalee pointed to two of his men, who were still mounted. "You two, go check those brands." They wheeled their mounts and rode off after the cattle. A few minutes later they returned and reported. "It's hard to tell," the older rider said. "The brands are fresh, but they could've been altered. "Only way to tell for sure, is to skin a couple steers and see what it looks like on the other side of the hide."

"Well then, do it. Take a couple more men to help you. When you get hides, bring them into town."

"You butcher my cattle, Parmalee and the town's going to have to pay for them," Stacy warned. "You won't find any altered brands on my cattle."

"We'll see about that," Parmalee said with amusement. "In the meantime, I'm taking you, Slate and Carlin in. I don't have jail cells enough for all of your punchers, so I'm letting them go for now. Let them know right now, they are not to cause any trouble, or it will go bad for all of you."

THE DEVIL'S JUSTICE

Stacy glanced around at her men. "You heard the Sheriff, boys," she said. "Any of you who don't want any part of trouble and want to clear out of the country, it's all right with me. Tell Zeke Austin what happened and tell him I said to pay you off. Anyone who wants to stay,..stay. But, no trouble. Understand? I'll be back."

"I wouldn't count on it," the sheriff chuckled.

THE DEVIL'S JUSTICE

Chapter Six

It was almost dusk when Parmalee and his posse rode into town with their prisoners. Holt and his men had separated from the posse, half way back to town, and had returned to the Rafter H, as their further assistance had not been needed. The wounded posse member was taken to Doc Finch to be looked after.

Townspeople all stopped to stare and watch the procession of weary riders as they rode into town and reined to a halt in front of the sheriff's office. John and Amy Parker came out of their newspaper office and watched from the porch.

The sheriff dismissed his posse, except for his regular deputy, and the riders disbursed and rode off , going their separate ways, back to living their own separate lives.

Once inside the Sheriff's office, Stacy Merritt, Morgan Slate, and Jace Carlin were ushered to the back where two jail cells were located. There was a disheveled old man, sleeping off a drunk in one of them. The cell door was still open. The old man snored heavily.

"Alright, Percy," the deputy said, shaking the old drunk awake. "Time to get up. You gotta go now."

The old man murmured something unintelligible and tried to roll over and go back to sleep.

THE DEVIL'S JUSTICE

"C'mon. C'mon," the deputy said, pulling the old man to his feet and dragging him out of the cell, leading him to the front door.

"Alright, Miss Merritt," Parmalee said, indicating the empty cell by brandishing the barrel of the six gun toward it. "Inside."

She glared at him as she stepped inside without a word. "And you Slate, you're in that cell. He shoved him forcefully through the open door of the other cell.

Jace Carlin, willingly started to follow him in, but Will Parmalee grasped his arm and pulled him back. "Not you, Jace. I don't think it would be too safe for you to be locked up with this pair."

"You've got that right, Sheriff ," Slate sneered. "I'd kill that little traitor."

Parmalee ignored the threat. "Jace," he said. "I don't know how you got mixed up in this and I can't lock you up with these two, so I'm letting you go for now. But, stick around until this thing has been settled. You're not out of the woods yet."

"You don't have to pretend, Sheriff," Stacy said. "We know this is all a set up. Carlin's in this with you and Holt. You never had any intention of holding him."

"Think what you want," Will said, locking the cell doors without looking at either of his captives. Then to Carlin, he said, "Go on, Jace. Get out of here."

Jace looked the sheriff over warily. He started to say something, but thought better of it, so he turned on his heel and started for the front door.

THE DEVIL'S JUSTICE

"Better give the little man, his gun back, Parmalee," Morgan chided. "He's gonna need it when I get out of here."

"Who says you're going to get out," Parmalee retorted. He turned to Jace.

"Your gun and holster are on the desk. You'd better take them on your way out."

Morgan Slate was still laughing when Jace closed the door behind him.

Carlin was just starting to mount his horse when a man's voice sounded behind him from down the street. "Jace!"

Carlin turned and saw John Parker approaching. The man was trying to hurry, but Jace could see that the man's age had slowed him down to a forced shuffle. He was still wearing his printer's apron. He held out his right hand, ready to greet Jace as he approached. "I'm sorry I didn't get to talk to you when you came into town the other day. It's good to see you again"

Jace took the old man's hand and held it briefly, then released it. "Good to see you, John," He fought the urge to smile at seeing his old friend again, but he was feeling wary of everyone right now. "But, it seems, you're the only one who doesn't make it plain that things would be better if I hadn't showed up."

"Then I won't pretend either, Jace," Parker said. There was fear in his hazel eyes. "There's only trouble here for you. There's nothing the rest of us can do about it. We have to live here. You can just ride on. We can't."

THE DEVIL'S JUSTICE

Jace eyed him quizzically. "What are you talking about, John?" He asked. "You mean the trouble with the Diamond 8?"

Parker started to respond, but his face suddenly grew dark and the lines in his face deepened as his gaze passed over Carlin's left shoulder. Jace turned his head and saw Will Parmalee emerging from his office onto the boardwalk. "Talk to Russ Shaw," he said quickly in a low conspiratorial voice; the scurried away toward the Sheriff.

"Will!" He said excitedly as he approached. "Got a story for me?" He asked with forced expectancy.

The last thing Jace Carlin wanted to do, was to see Russ Shaw again. He could never forget that Shaw, then the county sheriff, had refused to stand up to the men who had murdered his family and destroyed his home. He told himself that he hated the man for forcing him to go after the outlaws himself, but deep down, Jace Carlin knew that he, alone, wanted to be the man who would track down these killers and mete out justice to them. Justice, he thought. Was it? Or was it the Devil's Justice, after all? An empty, unsatisfying, unquenchable thirst for vengeance.

He forced the thought away as he reined the mare up in front of Russ Shaw's one story cottage, just outside of town. Jace remembered when the place was well kept up with flowers and shrubs and a quaint white picket fence. But, now the property was run down and shabby looking. The house was long overdue for repainting and what was left of its original white coat, was now gray and dirty; peeling off against the elements. The place was overrun with weeds and what was left of the picket fence was bare and rotted.

He dismounted, passed through the gate that was hanging by only one hinge and stepped up onto the rotting porch. As he raised his fist to knock on the door, he felt a sudden urge to turn back and ride away. He started to follow this urge, but something told him not to. He quickly forced himself to knock. Almost hoping he would not be heard, he only rapped lightly at first. He waited several seconds. No answer. He told himself to go and he felt relief. But just as he started to move away, the door swung open.

The woman standing in the doorway was tall and thin. Her lined and wrinkled face was almost as gray and colorless as her thinning straight hair that was pulled back in a bun and tied at the nape of her neck. "What do you want?" She said angrily. "We've got no use for you here. Haven't you hurt my husband enough already?"

"John Parker sent me," Jace said quietly in defense.

"Can't imagine why," she said haughtily. "But that makes no difference to me, no how. Best you be on your way." She started to close the door in his face.

"Let him in, Sarah," a gravelly voice from inside called.

She stiffened, then swung the door open reluctantly, she continued to glare at him.

"Thank you, ma'am," he choked over the lump in his throat as he stepped inside.

THE DEVIL'S JUSTICE

There was a small living room just beyond the vestibule. Russ Shaw was sitting in a Morris chair next to the pot bellied stove. Light filtered in from the kitchen, but otherwise Russ Shaw was sitting in the dark.

"I heard you were back," Shaw said gruffly. "Wondered how long it would take you to get around to me."

Shaw had been a big man, the last time Jace had seen him, but now the man was just a shadow of his former self. He looked withered and old. His thick brown mustache had turned to pure white to match what was left of his hair. He wore wire rim glasses and his hands were bony and gnarled.

"Heard a lot about you, Carlin. How you tracked those boys down and shot them one by one. Made a big name for yourself, haven't you? Now you're here for me, aren't you? You're going to finish what you started? Well go ahead boy, get it over with."

Jace could see the complacency, the resolve, and lack of fear in the old man's eyes, through the thick lenses of his spectacles.

"I haven't got anything to finish," Jace said flatly. "It's already finished," he almost growled, anger welling up inside of him. Anger at the old man for failing to do his job. And anger at himself for feeling no compassion for this sick, burned out former lawman.

"And now you're satisfied," the old man said.

"No. I'm not."

"Just what is it you want then?" He said as if he really didn't care. "Why'd you come here?"

THE DEVIL'S JUSTICE

"Look, old man," Carlin said. "I never wanted to see you again, but John Parker said you wanted to see me. So here I am."

"Why would I want to see you?" The old man scoffed.

"I don't know. John said I should talk to you."

"That's not the same as me wanting to talk to you."

"No," Jace admitted. Maybe he had just made an assumption. "I guess it isn't." Then he added. "I guess I made a mistake. I never should have come here."

"No you shouldn't have," Shaw said bluntly. "You never should've ever come back to Contention Springs in the first place. If you have any sense left, you'll ride on and forget about this town."

"Can't do that. I want my ranch back. I intend to stay here."

"And do what? Kill some more? That's the only way you're ever going to get that land back." He half chuckled and half sneered. "Hell, you'll have to keep killing to keep it, even if you did get it back."

Carlin's eyes narrowed and his brow furrowed. "Just what the hell is going on around here? Everyone's so mysterious about things. What's everybody afraid of?"

"You really don't know do you?" The old man said, evenly. "Then you're a bigger fool than I ever thought you were." He shoved himself straighter in his chair and glowered. "Now get the hell out of here and leave me be." He turned his head away, refusing to look at Carlin any more.

Carlin's jaw tightened and he refrained from talking back. He turned quickly on his heel. He ignored Mrs. Shaw, who had been standing behind him watching and listening, as he passed her by, jerked the front door open and left brusquely.

It was completely dark, now as he mounted the mare and neck reined her around to head back toward the middle of town. The night air was crisp and had turned cool, contrasting sharply with the heat of anger, he was feeling at the back of his neck. He rode slowly along the main street, his thoughts consuming his consciousness and blotting out the night sounds of crickets and locusts. The tinny sounds of pianos and fiddles emanating from the two local saloons soon filled the air. The street was empty save for the glow of lights from open establishments and the evenly spaced street fires that provided night light along the thoroughfare.

Carlin had just passed the hardware store and was approaching the saloons, when.........

"Carlin!" The voice was sharp and menacing, behind him. He jerked hard on the reins, pulling the mare's head high. The animal dance about in place at the sudden restraint and half turned as Carlin twisted in the saddle, turning toward the voice.

Slate Morgan stood in the middle of the street, legs spread shoulder width apart. Both hands were filled with shooting irons. The glow of the street light fires danced in his dark eyes and the barrels of his pistols. Instinctively, Jace pulled harder on the reins. The mare swiveled, in place, on her hind haunches, and twisted around and rearing high lifting her front legs off the ground and pawing at the air.

Flame stabbed from the muzzles of Slate's guns, followed by the sound of simultaneous crashings. spewing clouds of thick powder smoke filling the crisp night air. A slug whipped past Carlin's left ear. Only the sudden movement of his horse saved him from a direct hit, but the gray mare took the second slug directly in its eye. The horse screamed in agony, thrashing about; her legs collapsing beneath her, and tumbling to the ground. Jace pitched sideways, half leaping from the saddle, as Slate continued shooting. Slugs streaked passed Carlin's falling figure, through the night air; some thudding into the wall of the Hardware Store while others smashed the large plate glass windows.

Pain shot throughout Jace's body as he fell against the hitchrail; his rib cage smashing against the cross bar. The rail splintered beneath his falling weight and Jace landed against the edge of the board sidewalk. Ignoring the pain, he pushed himself in one swift movement away as the big body of the mare plunged and fell against the rubble. The splintered uprights of the hitch rail plunged into the animal's side and momentarily held the great body partly off the ground before the weight finally let the dying horse slide the rest of the way to the ground.

Bullets thudded into the side of the horse as Morgan Slate continued firing; moving forward quickly with the confidence of victory. The falling horse had shielded Jace, just long enough for him

THE DEVIL'S JUSTICE

to roll away, pitch forward off the walk away from the downed horse; drawing his own pistol as he clambored half way to his feet and dove behind a water trough.

Slate saw the movement and swung his guns towered Carlin's hiding place. Firing rapidly, with first one hand and then the others, at the water trough, the gunman stalked steadily forward; his pistol spouting flame amidst thundering claps of his volley. . Streams of water spurted through the holes and wood chunks chipped, splintered and flew into the air.

Jace dived away from the trough, rolling out into the street. Bullets stitched the ground before him, barely missing him as he rolled away. As he rolled to his back, and pushed himself slightly upward, a slug tore through the top of his shirt sleeve and burned the his shoulder. At the same instant he raised his pistol and fired.

Slate halted suddenly, as if stunned. His dark eyes widened with surprise and a crimson blotch spread over his broad chest. As realization set in, what had happened, he thumbed back the hammers of his Colts one more time, but it was too late. Carlin had pushed himself to a sitting position and his gun arm was pushed straight out in front of him; his fist grasping his pistol firmly. His eye squinted along the barrel, placing the gunsights squarely on Slate's middle. The weapon bucked and belched flame. The bullet ripped into Slate's belly, tearing a massive hole. He fell backward a step as Carlin's next shot made the hole bigger. He bent over, dropping his guns and trying to grasp his wounds with his hands, but he couldn't move. His eyes glazed over and his knees sagged beneath him. Carlin poured two more slugs into the gunman's bullet riddled body as Slate sank to his knees and then pitched face downward into the dirt and rolled over onto his back.

Carlin pushed himself to his feet and slowly approached the fallen man, keeping his pistol aimed at the fallen man. His eyes flamed with fury. His jaws clenched, trying to contain his rage. His face was a mask of cold grimness. To his right the mare was in the final throes of agony; legs kicking spasmodically, sides pumping up and down as the animal gasped for breath and wheezing with a shrill mournful sound.

In front of him, lie Morgan Slate; his chest chewed apart and covered with blood. He too, writhed and moaned in agony. Carlin gazed coldly down at the dying gunman. He felt nothing. No remorse; not even hate. Just nothing.

"Finish me off, Carlin," Slate choked. "I can't stand it any more. Why don't you end it? Please!" His arms wrapped around his middle and he rocked back and forth.

Carlin said nothing. Only stared for a moment, lifted his pistol, turned on his heel and turned to the dying mare. "Sorry, old girl," he said sadly. He placed the muzzle of his gun barrel behind the horse's ear, thumbed back the hammer and squeezed the trigger. As the roar of the pistol echoed in the street, the mare relaxed and went silent.

Carlin slid his gun into its holster and turned to walk away, down the street.

THE DEVIL'S JUSTICE

"What about me, Carlin?" He heard Slate plead.

Without turning to look back, Carlin said, "You can go to hell." He continued walking away.

Townspeople were gathering in the street now. Doc Finch and several others hurried toward the dying gunslinger. Will Parmalee had emerged from his office and was striding quickly toward Carlin. John and Amy Parker watched intently from the porch in front of the print shop.

"What was he doing out of jail?" Jace snapped as Parmalee came close.

"Nothing to hold them on," he said quickly and nervously. "The men brought in the hides. Showed the brands had not been run over. They were Diamond H cattle alright."

"Then I guess you're going to have to pay her for those steers, after all." He gazed over the sheriff's shoulder and could see Stacy Merritt sitting astride her horse, in the shadows, a bit further down the street. She met his stare for a moment, then angrily turned her mount and rode swiftly out of town.

Will ignored the jibe. "Morgan dead?"

"If he's not yet, he will be," Jace said flatly. "He didn't give me a choice. He opened fire on me first. Shot my horse. She was a good horse. We've ridden a lot of trails together. She didn't deserve it."

"No," Will agreed. "And I'm not blaming you, Jace. You'll get no trouble from me. But, a word of friendly advice. Ride on. This is no place for you any more."

THE DEVIL'S JUSTICE

"Can't do that. I'm staying to get my spread back."

"Even if it means more killing?"

"I guess I really don't care much anymore," Jace said evenly.

"You really have become one cold hearted son of a bitch, haven't you, Jace?"

"Yes, I have."

He pushed past the sheriff and strode away.

THE DEVIL'S JUSTICE

Chapter Seven

"Jace!" Jenna Holt exclaimed with surprise and excitement. She stood framed in the door, backlit by the light of the lamps inside the house. She smiled broadly and her eyes danced with delight. "What brings you here this time of night?" She blushed. "I mean, of course you're welcome here any time. Oh, I am so glad to see you, but is there something wrong?" She saw the grimness on his face and he was somewhat stooped with the pain of his bruised ribs.

Before he could answer, he could hear Duncan Holt from the living room. "Come in Jace," he called, putting down his book on the small table next to the stuffed chair he was sitting in.

Jenna, backed quickly aside as Jace stepped brusquely inside. Even in the vestibule, Jace could smell the aroma from Duncan's pipe. He stopped in the archway leading to the living room. Jenna stood behind him, in anticipation. Duncan could see the seriousness in Carlin's demeanor. "Something wrong?" Duncan asked.

"No. Morgan Slate is dead."

Holt jumped to his feet. There was a pleased expression on his face and his lips curled into a half smile of amazement. "How…..?

Jace anticipated his concern and answered. "In town in front of everyone, including the sheriff. He started it. I finished it."

"Very good, Jace," he said. "Perfect."

Even though Slate had it coming, somehow, Jace didn't like the satisfaction that Duncan seemed to be enjoying. "So," Jace said, getting right to the point. "I get my spread back, right."

Holt shrugged turned and walked to the writing desk in the corner. He lowered the door that opened flat into a writing surface. He rummaged through the small drawers inside until he found what he was looking for. Jace waited expectantly while Holt sorted out what he wanted.

Disappointment and anger spread over Carlin's face as Holt turned to face him. Jace had been expecting a deed, but Holt held out a sheaf of green back bills. "Six thousand, I believe was the agreement."

"Six thousand for the land," Jace said warily. "I'd only have to give the money back for payment, so why don't we skip the cash and get right to the deed?" He had a sudden dread of what was coming, and he wasn't wrong.

"The deal was six thousand for Morgan Slate. Not the land." Holt said smugly.

"I don't want the money," Jace snarled. "I want my land."

"Take the money, Jace," Duncan urged. "You've earned it."

"Earned it?'

"Of course. I hired you for a job and you did it. Most satisfactorily, I might add."

THE DEVIL'S JUSTICE

"I'm no hired gun," Jace protested angrily, stepping close to Holt almost, close enough to breath in the smoke from his pipe.

"Of course, you are," Holt chided. He let the bills slide from his palm. They fluttered to the carpet. "You're nothing more than a hired gun and a killer. Now pick up your money and get out."

Carlin's jaw clenched tighter. He stared threateningly into Holt's face for several seconds. Holt pursed his lips and stifled a smile. He was enjoying this.

Jace cursed himself for being taken in by Duncan Holt and he knew Holt was right. He was nothing more than a hired gun, afterall. So he made up his mind. Carefully, Jace bent his knees, lowering himself slowly to the floor. Keeping a furtive eye on Holt, he swept the bills together and folded them into a roll as he carefully stood up. He tucked the roll inside his left shirt pocket and buttoned the flap.

Then, without change of expression or warning, Jace's right arm came up lightning fast, driving his mallet like fist into Holt's face, smashing his nose and loosening his two upper front teeth. Holt fell backward against the fireplace mantle, bumped the back of his head and slid to the floor in a sitting position. His hand groped for his bloody face and his fingers came away red and sticky. Duncan's smugness had disappeared, replaced by shocked awe and fear.

"You're right," Carlin agreed. "I am just a hired gun."

THE DEVIL'S JUSTICE

He turned and stalked past Jenna and went out the door. He thought he detected a slight hint of amusement in Jenna's eyes.

Jace Carlin had slept late and it was midmorning before he arose and ventured out of his hotel room. He had been totally exhausted by the time he had returned to town the night before and returned the rented horse he had used to ride out to the Rafter H, to the livery stable. He had fallen into bed with his clothes on, too tired to worry about the pain of his bruised ribs and his anger with Duncan Holt.

The pain and the anger returned as sleep wore off and he became conscious of the bright morning sun streaming through the window of his hotel room. He cursed himself for trusting Duncan Holt and making himself an enemy with Stacy Merritt. Somehow, he was going to have to recitfy the situation. But how? Returning to the Diamond 8 would not be a smart thing to do. Stacy Merritt had shot at him the last time he had ridden onto her range. Next time, Jace was certain, that she wouldn't just put a bullet in his hat as warning. She would surely shoot to kill .No questions asked, no answers wanted. And he couldn't blame her. He knew she was convinced that he was in with Duncan Holt and had set up Morgan Slate to come after him, so the gunman could be done away with legally. Jace, now, knew he was the one that had been set up. He had thought Duncan Holt was his friend, but, he had been deceived. Holt had shown himself to be a ruthless man. If he would treat an old friend the way he treated Jace, maybe he was the one causing all the trouble in the valley. Still, Stacy Merritt had been the first to bring in a hired gun, and perhaps Duncan was merely fighting back. But why would he treat Jace that way? True, he had possession of Carlin's ranch and he wanted to keep it. Was it worth betraying a friend for it, though? Apparently.

Carlin was totally confused, desperately trying to figure out just what the situation was. Who was the aggressor and who was the victim. He had just about decided that both sides were equally guilty. The one defining factor was that Duncan Holt had his property and he wanted it back He knew he couldn't fight Holt alone. That meant that he would have gain Stacy Merritt's trust and to side with her, if it was at all possible. After the way he had already messed things up, he doubted that he could ever win her over. He would have to try though, even if it meant that she would kill him first.

Moving slowly and stiffly; his hand held tightly against his aching ribs, he had descended the hotel stairs. The pain was too much for him to think of food, so he passed by the hotel's dining room, crossed the lobby and went outside to the street. He pretended not to notice people staring at him, moving away and avoiding him; all the while regarding him with an almost revered, but fearful respect.

Down the street, Will Parmalee had just emerged from the newspaper office with Amy Parker. He had just given her a quick kiss on the cheek and he had left her standing on the porch while he crossed the street to his office. He didn't notice Jace Carlin watching him. But Amy Parker did. She turned and gazed down the street in Jace's direction. She lifted her skirts above her shoes and hurried toward him. Jace shuffled forward to meet her.

As the distance between them narrowed, Amy noticed how slowly he moved and she could see the pain in his eyes. Her first instinct was to feel for his pain, but she fought back the urge to say anything, lest she forget to say what she really wanted to talk to him about.

"I see you're still here. Will said he told you to move on," she said curtly

"And now you're telling me, is that it?"

"No. I'm asking you to. For your own good and everyone else's. If you stay, there will only be more killing. Maybe next time you won't walk away with just some bruises."

"Jace," she said, softening her tone. "Alice was a good friend to me. I know she wouldn't like to see what's happened to you. For her memory, just go away and stop this awful killing business."

"It is for her memory that I came back. And that's why I have to stay."

"No!" Amy snapped. "You want to stay so you can fight and kill again. You're not the Jace Carlin we use to know. You're just a cold heartless killer."

"Well, it seems you're in agreement with everyone else; including me." He tipped his hat to her and strode away toward the Sheriff's office.

Will Parmalee didn't look surprised when the door opened and Carlin stepped in. "You're not good at taking advice, Jace," he said non chalantly and turned his attention back to the newspaper he was reading. "I saw you ride out of town last night. I hoped you were leaving."

"You knew better than that, didn't you, Will?" Jace sneered. He stood silently before Will's desk, staring down at him. After a few moments, Parmalee peeked out from behind his paper, grimaced and threw it aside. "All right," he demanded with irritation, "What is it?"

"I rode out to the Rafter H last night."

"Didn't get your ranch back, did you?" Parmalee smirked knowingly. "I told you to forget about it when you first came to town. You didn't listen."

"You didn't tell me Duncan Holt had moved onto my spread."

"I didn't want to add disillusionment to your pain. I knew you thought Holt was your friend."

"What's happened to Duncan? He didn't use to be like this."

"Oh, you're wrong there, Jace. He's always been a selfish son of a bitch. He was just always good at conning everyone."

"I'm surprised to hear that from you. I thought you were on his side."

"My job is to keep the peace. As long as Duncan Holt gets his way, that makes my job easier."

"What about Stacy Merritt?"

"She's just trying to hold on to what's hers."

"But she brought in a hired gun. And what about Randy Poole?" Jace said.

"There was no proof that she had anything to do with Randy Poole's death. As for bringing in a hired gun, it seems to me that Holt brought in his own hired gun." The meaning was strong in Parmalee's eyes.

"Meaning me?" Carlin said bitterly.

"Yes. Meaning you."

"Then you knew it was a set up to force Morgan Slate into a gunfight."

"Of course."

"And you went along with it."

"Like I said, as long as Duncan gets his way. Besides, what's one less gunman to me?"

"Even though he might have killed me instead?" Jace remarked flatly.

"Like I said, what's one less gunman to me?" His gaze remained level on Carlin's face. There was a hint of a chuckle in his voice.

Jace remained silent. He guessed he had it coming.

"I understand you've been talking to Russ Shaw," Parmalee said, changing the subject.

"I suppose you could call it that," Jace said. "Neither one of us had much of anything to say to each other."

"Well, neither do we, Jace. I've already said all I've got to say. There's nothing I can do to help you. Stay around here and I can't be responsible for what happens to you."

"That's alright," Jace said. "You don't have to be. I can handle it myself." He turned on his heel and made for the door.

"I'm sure you can, Jace Carlin," the sheriff said as Carlin closed the door behind him.

THE DEVIL'S JUSTICE

The buggy and team passed him by in the street. Jenna holt pulled the matched team to a halt, turned on the seat and waited for Jace to catch up. He glanced angrily at her, then stared straight ahead and continued to walk on by.

"Jace!" She called. "I need to talk to you."

Carlin halted and looked up at her. "I don't think we have anything to talk about. Duncan already made it clear that you're not my friends."

"You're right, Jace. Duncan is not your friend. He's not anyone's friend. Not even mine," she said with a hurried clipped frenzy. Then her voice softened. "But I'm still your friend, Jace. I've always cared about you. You know that."

When he didn't answer back, she said, "Go for a ride with me. I've got something to tell you."

Jace thought better of it and told himself not to get suckered into something he would be sorry for. "Please," she pleaded. "It's important."

He started to walk on. She said quickly, "If you want your land back, ride with me." She waited for his answer.

"Alright," was all he said and climbed into the carriage.

Jenna whipped up the reins and clucked to the horses. Neither Jace nor Carlin spoke as they rode through town. Jace felt uneasy as he noticed townspeople watching. Jenna seemed to be ignoring them.

When they reached the edge of town, Jenna turned the team onto the east fork in the road. Only the sound of the horses' hooves and creak of wagon wheels prevailed until they were well out of town into the country. Jenna pulled the team off to the side of the road and parked the buggy in the shade of a large sycamore tree.

Jace waited for her to start the conversation. Finally she said, "I want to help you Jace."

"And what do you want from me in return?" He said coolly.

"Do you have to be so cynical? There was a time when we were close. Don't you remember?"

"Yeah, I remember," he said somberly.

"It could be that way again," she said plaintively.

"Seem to me you already have a man."

"If you can call him that," Jenna said. "He's changed a lot over the years. Greed has gotten the better of him. He's become ruthless and hungry for wealth and power."

"I've been told that he's always been like that."

"Yes, but I didn't recognize it at first." Then she said, "You didn't either. You still thought he was your friend up until last night. Now you know better too."

Jace nodded his agreement with a grimace.

"You want your land back and I want to be rid of him. Together we can both get what we want." She emphasized the word 'together' and the meaning was clear. "Without Duncan, you can have your land back, maybe even the Rafter H if you want it."

"Meaning you and me."

"Yes", she almost whispered.

"In other words, you want me to kill him?"

"Well, I wouldn't want to put it that bluntly. But yes, I guess so."

THE DEVIL'S JUSTICE

"So you're hiring me, is that it?"

"No. I was thinking of a partnership. A partnership of a permanent nature."

"I guess the price of my gun is getting more expensive," he mused.

"Don't look at it that way, Jace."

"How else should I look at it? First your husband hires my gun, then you hire it. I don't guess you're both wrong about me."

"What do you mean?"

"I'm just a hired gun afterall."

Stacy Merritt, Zeke Austin and a half dozen Diamond 8 riders were in town when Jace Carlin hoofed back into town.

He had wanted to walk back rather than have Jenna drive him back. He had told her it would be best if they were not seen together, any more than necessary, but the truth of the matter was he was angry. Angry at Jenna Holt's cold blooded plan and angry at himself for agreeing to it. But this would be the only way to get his ranch back The law was not going to help him and once again, if he were to get justice, he would have to mete it out himself, even if it was the Devil's Justice. It was better than no justice at all, he told himself. Or, maybe Amy Parker was right. Maybe he only wanted his land as an excuse to fight and kill again.

When he had ridden into Contention Springs a few days ago, he had told himself that he wanted the killing behind him, but did he really? He had already killed again; leaving Morgan Slate dying in the middle of the street and now he was planning to kill Duncan Holt.; a man he had once trusted and had called friend. Would the killing end with Duncan Holt? There was still the Diamond 8 to contend with and what about Will Parmalee?

Stacy Merritt and Zeke Austin were just emerging from the Sheriff's office when Jace spotted them. Their men had been waiting outside on their horses. Stacy and Zeke climbed into their saddles and started to turn them when they noticed Carlin in the street. Stacy said something to her men and they reined steady. She nodded to Zeke and they both urged their mounts forward toward the walking man.

As they neared him, Jace could see the anger in Stacy's eyes and the grimness in Zeke Austin's expression. They reined to a halt in front of him, blocking his path. "I'm surprise at you, Jace," The old man said gruffly. "Throwing in with Duncan Holt."

"It was mistake, Zeke," Jace said apologetically. "He lied to me. I know that now."

"Seems to me, you've whistled that tune before," Stacy Merritt put in angrily.

"Just a minute, Stace," Zeke urged calmly, holding his palm up in a halting fashion. "Let's hear what the boy's got to say. Then you can horsewhip him if you like, but right now let him have his say."

Stacy settled back in the saddle. Her eyes flashed. "He's got one minute," she sputtered.

"Alright, boy," Zeke said. "Let's have it."

"Duncan told me you were rustling cattle and driving everyone out of the valley," He said quickly. "I was already believing that you were the one who stole my place. I saw cattle with Diamond 8 brands there."

"It was Duncan Holt that took over your land," Stacy Merritt came back.

"I know that now," Jace said. "He offered me a way to get it back."

"Meaning Morgan Slate?" Zeke put in.

Jace nodded. "Yes," he said.

"But he didn't give it back to you, did he?" Stacy chided.

"I always thought he was my friend." There was sadness and disappointment in the words.

"I'm sorry I never said anything about it, before, son," Zeke said. "Duncan's always been a sneak. I just never wanted to be the one to tell you. I figured you'd find it out soon enough."

"Guess I never was very smart," Jace said.

"No boy, you just liked to see the good in people. You always wanted to give them a fair shake and the benefit of the doubt."

"Not anymore, Zeke." Carlin's eyes narrowed. He stepped around them and walked away.

THE DEVIL'S JUSTICE

Chapter Eight

The last golden rays of the retreating afternoon splintered into sharp needles; the last remains of the shards still above the horizon casting reflections of burned crimson and copper into the grayness of early evening sky. Dark clouds streamed lonely trails above, announcing the coming of crisp nighttime air.

Jace Carlin lay flat on his stomach in the high grass on top of a ridge overlooking the trail below. He held his head low, keeping concealed but raised just enough to see the trail. He arms were outstretched forward and a Winchester rifle was held firmly in his grasp: the stock pressed firmly into the hollow of his shoulder. His hands felt sweaty and clammy. Perspiration dripped from his brow and trickled into the corners of his eyes. Occasionally he would release his grip on the weapon and wipe the eyes clear. He felt a sickness in his gut and he fidgeted uneasy in the grass.

He had never cold bloodedly shot anyone without giving them a chance, much less an out and out bushwhack. What had happened to him? He tried not to think about it. Had he finally crossed over that line and become a killer, after all? No better than the men who had enraged him to a life of vengeance and violence.

THE DEVIL'S JUSTICE

He had been here in the grass for almost half an hour. As planned, he waited for Duncan Holt's buggy to appear. Jenna was to convince Duncan to drive her to town for a church function. Jace would ambush him from the ridge and then ride to town. Jenna would wait awhile to give Jace enough time to get to town ahead of her. That way Jace would have an alibi for his whereabouts at the time of the shooting. The assumption would be that someone from the Diamond 8 was responsible.

Jace hated to put the blame on Stacy Merritt or any of her riders, but it would keep him in the clear. Besides, it would be difficult to prove anything anyhow. He told himself it didn't matter. But why did it nag at him? Why did he hate Jenna Holt so much for conceiving such a plan? And why did he hate himself for going along with it?

For his home, he told himself. It belonged to him. Duncan Holt was only getting what he deserved.

The last remains of the sun were settling below the horizon. Dusk was setting in and the air became cooler and fresh. Crickets and locusts began their nighttime songs of loneliness. Jace strained his eyes to see into the distance along the trail Waiting. Heart beating excitedly. Beads of sweat standing out on his brow, yet not cooling him in the evening dampness.

Minutes ticked by and still no sign of the carriage. He slapped at hovering mosquitoes and punkies were biting his skin. Maybe, Jenna had lost her nerve, he thought. No. Not a chance. She was too cold. What had he seen in her years ago,

THE DEVIL'S JUSTICE

he wondered. How could she be Alice's sister and be so different?

Maybe she had failed to convince Duncan to drive out tonight. Maybe Duncan was smart enough to know Jenna had something planned. After all, a lot of townspeople had seen them riding together that day. Maybe word got back to Duncan somehow. Maybe……..

Then there it was. A dark shape was moving along the trail. It seemed to grow larger as it approached until finally, Carlin could make it out as a carriage and a team of horses. His pulse started to race even faster and his sweaty palms slipped on the rifle barrel and trigger housing.

He could hear the wheels of the carriage crunching on the gravel trail and he could hear the harness and trapping of the team creaking, plainly now. They were almost directly below him. He raised the front sight of the muzzle and placed it on Duncan Holt's head. His hands started to tremble and the sight wavered off and on his target. He must calm himself, but why couldn't he? For once in his life he pointed a gun at a man and did not feel vengeance in his heart. For the first time he felt fear. Not the fear of another man, another gun, or of death itself. He felt the fear of himself and knew now what all the others who had gone down by his gun, had felt in their last moments of life.

Before him, he saw the faces of the men before him as his gun barked time and again; bodies left where they fell. "I'll kill you, when I grow up! I hate you! I hate you!" A little boy's voice rang in his head. He saw a woman holding her dead husband in the middle of the street and crying; her son hugging her desperately about the neck.

Jace's body was shaking uncontrollably, now and his strength seemed to evaporate. Desperately, he tried to pull his weapon under control; his sights still wavering. His trigger finger squeezed against the trigger and it seemed to take all of his energy to pull it back far enough to take up the slack. Slowly, it moved into place. Only a slight pressure more and the rifle would explode sending a deadly lead projectile into Duncan Holt's unsuspecting body.

But then his body went limp and he released his grasp on the weapon. He fell flat on his face in the grass and tears streamed down his cheeks and he sobbed convulsively while the carriage containing Duncan and Jenna Holt continued uneventfully along the trail.

Jace lay there for several minutes; his face buried in the tall grass, as if hiding from shame. He listened to the steady clip clop of Holt's team and creaking of carriage wheels crunching in the gravel as the sounds steadily faded away until they could be heard no more. Only the lonely sounds of the night remained.

Then, suddenly, panic swept over him; his mind racing with confusion as he finally realized the full extent of what he had almost done. With a burst of energy he loosed his grip on the rifle, bent his arms beneath him; palms flat on the grassy ground, and pushed himself to his feet. He turned and ran blindly toward his rented horse that he had left tethered in the bushes at the bottom of the hill. He vaulted into the saddle, landing heavily on the animal's back, yanking on the reins and twisting the horse's neck savagely and raking his spurs cruelly into his sides.

The horse shrieked shrilly and snorted in pain as it turned almost completely around in place; its iron shod hooves digging clods of turf from the ground and sending them spewing out from under him. Carlin pulled the animal straight, loosened the reins and kicked the horse forward into a fast gallop. Across the meadow below, up a low ridge and down into the next valley, Carlin pushed his mount as full speed; lashing the animal with the trailing ends of the reins. The horse gasped with laboring breath. Lather flecked and then foamed against the animal's withers, sides and haunches. Carlin didn't seem to care. He just kept pushing the horse mercilessly forward without purpose, not even aware of where he was going or why.

The horse began to slow. Carlin lashed at him with the reins, urging him on, but the animal was just too worn out. He began to falter, then stumbled, and fell forward on his knees. Jace flew forward over the horse's head and fell clear as the animal rolled over on its side; his legs flailing with the fall until his strength was totally depleted and he lay still, save for the heaving of his sides and the gasping breath. Jace rolled across the hard packed earth, his wind knocked out of him. The blow seemed to bring him back to his senses and he sat up in the grass; breathing heavily. His eyes seemed blurred at first and then as he brought the scene before him into focus. Remorse washed over him as he realized what he had done to his horse. He saw the foamed lather covering his hide and he saw the bloody scratches his spurs had left on the animal's flanks. He listened to the labored breathing and cursed himself for his brutality.

After several moments, the horse began to breathe more normally. His sides no longer heaved and the foam was drying in his hair. Eventually the horse stirred , rolled over and put his feet beneath him. In another moment the animal was on his feet. He shook his head and his hide rippled.

Jace came to his feet and approached the horse, reaching for the bridle. The horse threw its head high and backed away warily.

"Steady, old boy," Jace said softly and reassuringly. "I'm not gonna hurt you anymore." He slid the palm of his hand over the horse's muzzle and patted his neck. The horse steadied and accepted the pats. "I was a danged fool for treating you that way. I had no right to do that to you. Let's get you some water and some fresh grass. Then I'll see about getting you someplace where we can get some salve for your scratches."

Gently, Jace took the reins and walked off into the darkness leading the horse behind him.

"There's someone out there," Pete Brogan said to his companion as he squinted his eyes into the darkness, trying to make out the dark shapes moving toward them. Brogan and Cal Dwire had been standing guard at the Diamond 8 ranch house gate; each one positioned on each side and carrying loaded Winchesters in the crooks of their arms. "Better go tell Miss Merritt," he said to

Dwire. The younger man nodded and hurried off toward the ranch house.

"Who's out there!" Brogan shouted. "We don't like anybody prowling around the Diamond 8. You'd better git before you get plugged."

"Hold your fire." A voice from the darkness came back. "I'm here to see Stacy Merritt. I've got business with her."

The dark shapes turned into a man on foot leading a horse behind him.

"She didn't tell me she was expectin' visitors," Brogan answered, jacking a round into the chamber of his Winchester; the sound loud enough in the night air to declare a menacing warning.

"It's important that I see her. And my horse needs tending to," Jace Carlin retorted without slowing his stride forward. He didn't bother to address the fact that he wasn't expected, but he did hold his hands high with reins in his right as he led his horse forward.

"Stop right where you are stranger!" The guard warned him. "Take another step and I'll drill you sure."

Carlin halted. Beyond the guard, he could see a rectangle of light flash from the ranch house door as it opened and almost closed. Three shadows hurried along the path toward the gate. Pete Brogan glanced out of the corner of his eye and saw Stacy Merritt, Cal Dwire, and Zeke Austin approach.

"Who's out there, Pete?" Jace heard Stacy Merritt's voice.

THE DEVIL'S JUSTICE

"Some jasper says you was expectin' him," Brogran growled in a tone of disbelief.

"It's me. Jace Carlin. It's important that I talk to you." Jace shouted before the issue of expectation continued.

"What do you want?" She answered.

"It's important. And my horse needs tending to."

"Let him come on in, Stace," he heard Zeke Austin say advisingly. "Can't hurt to talk. Besides I never turn away a horse in need of tending."

"Alright. Come on in, but keep your hands high. My men will have you covered."

Jace moved forward slowly and halted at the gate. He could see Stacy Merritt's face the shadowed starlight. Pete Brogan stepped around behind him, still holding his rifle ready. He looked the horse over carefully and ran his fingers along the animal's hide. The hair was matted and stiff from dried foam. He felt the gouges in the animal's sides and the horse flinched at the touch. "This animal's been treated badly," Brogan said. He stepped around in front of Carlin. His voice took on an edge. "You do this?" He accused.

"I'm afraid I did," Jace confessed ashamedly.

"You oughtta be horsewhipped," Brogan said bitterly.

"You're right," Jace agreed. "I should."

"Cal," Zeke Austin said. "Take the man's horse to the stable and see to his needs, will ya."

"Since you're here for awhile," Stacy said. "You might as well come inside."

THE DEVIL'S JUSTICE

Dwire took the reins from Carlin's hand and led the horse away.

"So you think you can take Morgan Slate's place?" Stacy Merritt chided. She was seated in a stuffed chair in the living room, across from Carlin, who had been given a straight back kitchen chair. Zeke Austin lounged on the settee.

Jace Carlin had explained to Stacy and Zeke that he had come to the Diamond 8 to offer the services of his gun. He was sorry that he had deprived her of her hired gun by killing Morgan Slate. He had told her of his falling out with Duncan Holt and his desire to get his own ranch back. He emphasized that they had a mutual enemy in Duncan Holt and it would be advantageous to both of them to work together. He failed to mention Jenna Holt's offer and how close he had come to murdering her husband and his subsequent abuse of his horse.

"I can replace his gun. Yes," he said not sure if there was actually a relationship between Stacy Merritt and Morgan Slate that went beyond employer and employee. "And it won't cost you anything. I'll work for free. I just want to get my home back."

"You think I make a practice out of hiring gun men?" Stacy asked, then answered her own question. "Well I don't. I don't like killing."

"I don't either," Jace stated.

"You don't?" It wasn't a question. She raised her brow.

"No," Jace said flatly, but it sounded hollow to himself.

THE DEVIL'S JUSTICE

Stacy was thoughtful for a moment, then turned to Zeke as if for a comment.

"Might as well work together," Zeke advised. "It just might work out."

She turned back to Jace. "Alright, but no killing unless I approve. You understand that?"

"That the same arrangement you had with Slate?"

"Yes. And until you came along, he never had to use his gun."

"What about Randy Poole?" Jace asked.

"What about him?"

"You mean Slate didn't kill him?"

"No," she snapped. "I don't know who killed Randy Poole. I assumed Duncan Holt had something to do with it."

"Why would he do that? Randy worked for Holt. What reason would Duncan have to have to kill one of his own men?"

"I don't know. To blame it on me I suppose."

"Well to tell the truth," Jace said. "I sided with Holt, not just because I thought he was my friend, but because I was told that Randy was killed by Diamond 8. That made you the bad guys right there."

"Who told you that? Amy Parker?"

"Yes. Why would she lie about it?"

"I'm sure she believes it. Will Parmalee has been sparking Amy ever since Randy Poole's death. He's in Duncan Holt's pocket and of course he would blame it on us."

"I guess I've been wrong about a lot of things," Jace mused. "I'm sorry I ever sided against you." He didn't look at Stacy as he said it and she didn't respond either.

Seconds ticked off silently with no words spoken until the stillness was broken by the sound of hoofbeats approaching outside. By the sounds of it, a fairly large group of riders were approaching. Muffled sounds from the guards outside could be heard. The hoofbeats silenced and there was a rapping on the door. Cal Dwire was shouting, "Miss Merritt! Miss Merritt! The Sheriff and a posse are outside."

She swung the door open. Cal's arm was still raised and his fingers still fisted for pounding on the door. He stepped back quickly as Stacy Merritt pushed past him. Zeke Austin followed, putting his hat on as he went. Jace trailed slowly behind them in the shadows..

"What's going on, Sheriff?" Stacy demanded as she approached the mounted group of riders.

"We're looking for Jace Carlin," Will Parmalee said. "He murdered Duncan Holt tonight."

Jace froze in his tracks. He was several paces behind Stacy and Zeke and still in the shadows. He faded back slowly and slid around the corner of the ranch house and pressed him back against the wall, in deeper shadow, where he could listen. His pulse began to race. Duncan Holt dead? Had he actually shot the man without realizing it? No! What was happening? How could this be?

THE DEVIL'S JUSTICE

"What....?" Jace heard Stacy start to stammer. "That's impossible. Carlin may kill in a stand up fight, but not murder."

"You're barking up the wrong tree, Sheriff," Zeke Austin put in. "The boy just doesn't have it in him to out and out murder."

"You're wrong there," Parmalee said. "He waited on a ridge above the trail to town and ambushed him when he rode by in his carriage."

Jenna, Carlin thought to himself. She must have told Parmalee about the plan.

"I don't believe it," Zeke scoffed.

"There was a witness who saw it all," Parmalee retorted. "His wife was in the carriage with him."

Damn that cold hearted bitch! Jace cursed to himself. When Jace failed to do the job, she must have decided to do it herself and blame him for it.

"And you're taking her word for it?" Zeke said. "I wouldn't be surprised if she did it herself."

"That's nonsense. She's pretty distraught. She's staying in town with the Shaw's right now until she can settle down. Besides, it's not just her word alone. We found Carlin's rifle on the ridge where he waited in ambush."

Zeke started to say something, but Parmalee interjected. "And yes I'm sure it's his rifle. It's got his initials carved in the stock and I've seen him with it many times. What more proof do we need?" It wasn't a question demanding an answer.

What a fool he had been to leave the weapon behind, Jace told himself. Then he thought. But the bullet in Duncan Holt had not come from his rifle. Surely when the bullet that killed him didn't match with his rifle, he would be in the clear.

"Besides," Jace heard Parmalee say. "The rifle had one round gone and the weapon had been recently fired. The bullet that killed Holt came from a Winchester rifle."

Damn! Jace thought. His rifle had been used to kill Duncan Holt. But how was that possible? How could Jenna have gotten hold of his rifle? She couldn't. She must have had an accomplice. Someone to use as a back up if Carlin failed to do the job. Jenna was smart, he thought. She knew he couldn't do the job, and she wanted to set him up for the blame, anyways.

"What made you think he'd be here?" Jace heard Stacy ask.

"You were seen talking to him in town today. With Morgan Slate gone I thought you might have been trying to hire Carlin as his replacement."

"Best you don't try to think, Sheriff," Stacy snapped sarcastically. "That doesn't appear to be your forte."

"Fort-tay?" Parmalee looked perplexed.

"Don't try to figure it out, Sheriff. It's too big of a word for you anyhow. It's got all of five letters."

"Don't get smart with me, Missy," Parmalee said with annoyance. Then his tone became hard. "Well? Is he here or not?'

Stacy and Zeke both cast a furtive glance over their shoulders into the shadows behind them. Jace was nowhere to be seen. They both jerked their heads back to face the Sheriff and his posse.

THE DEVIL'S JUSTICE

"No. Of course not." Stacy was emphatic, but a hint of nervousness was in her voice.

Parmalee noticed the uneasiness and the glances toward the house. Deliberately he swung his right leg high, swinging it over his mount's back and slowly, but deliberately stepping down from the saddle. "Then you shouldn't mind if we just look around," he said. He handed the reins to the man sitting his horse next to him. "Sim," he said, not even looking at the man. "You stay here and hold the horses. Bill, Ed you come with me. The rest of you men spread out. Search the barn, corrals, and bunkhouse. If he's here, don't let him get away. Don't be afraid to shoot if you have to." He was already pushing Stacy Merritt and Zeke Austin aside and striding along the walk toward the front door. He drew his pistol and held it high.

Jace rolled further back into the shadows, keeping close to the ranch house wall and moving toward the back of the house. He could hear Will Parmalee's boot steps and chinking spurs louder as he came closer to the front door.

The door was still ajar and the Sheriff kicked the door open with the flat of his right foot. He burst through the doorway, waving his Colt back and forth. His eyes darting in unison with his pistol and seeking out any trace of movement.

At the same time, Jace scurried to the rear of the building and ran along the back wall to the other side of the ranch house.

Stealthily, he crept along the side wall toward the front corner of the ranch house. This side of the house was not in as much shadow as the other side and Carlin knew he could be spotted, even from a distance. He bent low and pressed close to the wall. He peered around the corner and saw the posse men spreading out searching the place. He saw one lone rider still atop his horse and holding the reins of the other horses.

He waited several moments until he saw some of the men enter the barn. His heartbeat throbbed dully in his head and perspiration beaded on his forehead, dripped down his cheek and off his chin. His mouth felt dry and his hands were moist and clammy. He had to make his move now and take his chances.

He lurched around the corner of the house. Taking long running strides as fast as he could push himself. With a leaping lunge, he threw himself forward and sideways, landing astride the lone rider's horse behind his saddle, landing heavily and startling the horse. The rider, taken by surprise, started to twist in the saddle, but found himself pushed mightily from the saddle to land spread eagled on the ranch house lawn.

Carlin pushed himself forward into the seat of the saddle taking up the reins, at the same time loosing the reins of the other horses. He whipped his mount around and kicked him forward into the bunch of other horses. He kicked at them with his feet still in the stirrups and let out whoops and yells to startle them into dispersing and running off.

At the sound, men came running out of the barn and bunkhouse. Others came running across the barnyard and Will Parmalee followed by two other men came running out of the house. Parmalee fired quickly without taking time to aim,

THE DEVIL'S JUSTICE

but the bullets whined close near Carlin's head. The other men followed suit and opened up with a volley of shots.

Carlin had already spun his horse around and kicked him into a gallop, following the running horses through the ranch's gate. The posse men came running after the man and horses, still firing as they ran until they too passed through the gate. They halted and kept firing for a few moments until they realized that Carlin was already too far out of pistol range.

Will Parmalee, held up his left hand as signal for his men to stop firing. He slammed his pistol angrily into his leather holster as he peered into the darkness, barely seeing the disappearing shadows of the running horses. Carlin had veered off from the frightened herd and headed north. "There's horses in the corral, men. It'll take a while to saddle up and he'll get a good lead on us. But we'll still get him."

It took an hour for Jace Carlin to reach Contention Springs. He had deliberately headed north away from the Diamond 8, knowing that when the posse was remounted they would head that way after him. They wouldn't expect him to circle back and head east toward town. As he approached town, it was already mostly in darkness as many of the establishments had closed down for the night. Even the two saloons were dark and quiet. Even with this much darkness, Carlin dared not chance being seen, so instead of riding directly into town, he circled wide, skirting the the main road and approached the town once again, but this time from the west.

As he came close to Russ Shaw's place, he guided his horse off the main road and came in behind the house. He noticed a faint flickering of light through a side window, indicating that someone was still up this late at night. In a stand of cottonwoods behind the house, he dismounted and tethered the horse to a young tree that had not yet grown thick. Swiftly and silently, he approached the rear of the house, climbed the rickety steps of the back porch and crept toward the back door. Loose boards creaked beneath his boots. Carefully, slowly, he pulled on the screen door. The top screen was loose and hanging down from an upper corner. The spring twanged lightly as it stretched with the opening of the door. Carlin gripped the back door's knob. It turned readily. Luck was with him. It was not locked.

As quietly as he could, he slipped through the doorway and closed the door behind him. He was standing in an alcove. It was dark here, but light from the living room and kitchen filtered through enough that he could see coats and hats hanging on the wall of the alcove. He could hear voices from the other room. They were low and he couldn't make out what was being said, but he did recognize Jenna Holt's voice among them.

Jace stepped forward out of the alcove. He had his gun out pointing at the Shaws and Jenna where they sat in their chairs. His eyes were cold and hard. The conversation ended abruptly as they saw the gunman step forward out of the shadows. Carlin remained silent.

THE DEVIL'S JUSTICE

"I suppose you've come for me," Jenna said haughtily. "First you kill my husband. Now you've come to finish me too."

"You're right, Jenna," Jace said. "I've come for you, but not to kill you. I'm taking you to Will Parmalee and you're going to tell him who really did kill Duncan."

'What's he talking about?" Russ Shaw said gruffly, staring at Jenna. He was still sitting in the same chair as he was during Carlin's first visit.

Jenna drifted her gaze away from the old man and glared at Jace.

"Go ahead, Jenna," Jace prodded. "Tell him how you plotted with me, to kill your husband for you. And when I didn't do it, you found somebody else to do it for you."

"You'll never prove that," Jenna retorted. "Besides, nobody's going to believe you. A hired killer."

"We'll see about that," Jace said. He came forward, pulled out a straight backed chair, sat in it and leaned his head back against the wall behind him. "Right now I just want everyone to be calm and patient. We're going to wait right here until Will Parmalee and his posse gets back. Then, I'm taking you in, Jenna."

"You never were very bright, Jace." Jenna laughed.

Chapter Nine

It was almost mid morning when Parmalee and his trail weary posse ambled into town and disbursed. The Sheriff had brought Stacy Merritt and Zeke Austin in with them and had jailed them for harboring and protecting a fugitive. He really had nothing to hold them on, but his hope was that he could flush Carlin out by coming to their aid. He had just settled them in to their cells when the front door opened. Parmalee's jaw dropped as Jenna Holt and Jace Carlin entered. He drew his pistol instinctively and aimed it at Carlin.

"You won't need that gun, Will," Jace said calmly. "There's been a mistake made, here and Mrs. Holt is going to clear it all up." He shoved her roughly and she stumbled forward toward the tall lawman.

Parmalee caught her with his left hand and prevented her from falling. He kept his weapon pointed at Carlin's chest.

She turned. Her eyes flashed angrily at Carlin. "You can't get away with pushing me around!" She blustered.

"Tell him, Jenna," Jace ordered. "Tell him who really killed Duncan."

She settled down and her scowl brightened to a smirking smile. "He did, Will." she pointed at Jace. "Just like I told you before. I saw him do it."

THE DEVIL'S JUSTICE

"Unbuckle your gunbelt, Jace," Parmalee ordered calmly.

"Wait a minute, there, Will," Jace pleaded. "If that were true, would I have come here?" He didn't wait for an answer. He continued. "Yesterday, she hired me to kill her husband. She offered to give my ranch back to me." He glared at Jenna. "I never should have agreed to it, but I wanted my home back."

"Then, you're admitting that you killed him?" Parmalee said

"No. I couldn't do it. I could never shoot anyone down from ambush. I know that now."

"You knew that too, didn't you?" He directed it to Jenna. "So you had a backup plan. You had someone else do the job and you blamed it on me."

"That sounds a bit far fetched," Will said flatly without looking at Jenna. There was a sly gleam in her eye that said, 'I told you so.' He remembered her warning him that nobody would believe a hired killer. It angered Carlin more and it was meant to.

"I came to you,Will, Because I thought you were a fair man. That you would hear me out and at least consider the truth. We used to be friends. Remember?"

"Yeah, I remember. And yes, we used to be friends. But that was before you went crazy and started killing people." Then to Jenna he said, "You go on and go home. I'll take care of Mister Carlin."

"Will, you can't let her go just like that," Jace started to protest.

THE DEVIL'S JUSTICE

"As I said before, Jace," Parmalee's voice took a harder edge. "Unbuckle your gun belt and let it drop." He eared back the hammer of his Colt and it clicked at full cock.

Carlin's eyes turned dark and cold. His hand drifted above his holstered sixshooter. His fingers curled.

"Don't try it, Jace," Will warned. "You'll never make it."

Carlin braced himself. Feet spread shoulder width apart.

"Jace! Don't do it! He'll kill you!"

Carlin was jolted out of his concentration. He jerked his head toward the voice and for the first time realized that Stacy Merritt and Zeke Austin were behind bars. "What are they doing in there?" Jace demanded.

"Aiding and abetting a fugitive," Will answered.

"That's crazy," Jace said. "They didn't know anything about this." Then he ordered defiantly, "Let them out!"

Will half grinned. "I will. Just as soon as you go inside and take their place. Now, what's it going to be? You going to give up your gun like I told you."

Jace glanced back to his friends in the cell. Stacy said, "Oh, Jace....."

Carlin thought about it for a moment. Seconds ticked by in silence. Then, he let out a breath and his body seemed to relax. His fingers moved away from his gun. Slowly he reached for his gunbelt buckle, let it loose and let the entire rig of gun and holster fall heavily to the floor.

THE DEVIL'S JUSTICE

"Now step back and let the lady pass," Parmalee brandished the muzzle of his weapon and nodded to Jenna.

Jenna glanced at Will and nodded. She lifted her long skirt an inch above the floor and started for the door. As she passed Carlin, she paused and flashed a smile of victory. Jace felt a sinking in his stomach and he clenched his jaw in anger and frustration as he watched her leave and close the door behind her.

The day had dragged on slowly. Jace Carlin brooded in his cell. How could he have been so stupid to think that all he had to do was to tell the truth and Jenna would be behind bars instead of himself? How could he have misjudged Will Parmalee so much? Or was it really himself that he had misjudged. Perhaps, he was no more than a hired killer whose word was no longer any good.

He had alternately been pacing the small area of his cell and occasionally throwing himself on the musty mattress of his bunk, trying to think things through; trying to come up with a solution to his predicament. He could think of nothing. He could hope for nothing. He had told Stacy Merritt and Zeke Austin to go home and not to try anything foolish, like trying to break him out of jail.

Now as he lay on the meager mattress staring up at the barred window of his cell, he watched the waning afternoon sunlight fade into dusk. Dark shadows invaded his tiny prison and he felt even more alone and abandoned.

THE DEVIL'S JUSTICE

He lay there alone in the darkness listening to the street sounds slowly diminish and replaced with the night sound of crickets, locusts, and peepers. He could hear the clink of a tin plate and utensils as the deputy on duty sat behind the desk and worked away at his supper. Carlin's own supper sat cooling on the floor just inside the door of his jail cell.

He heard the front door open and a shuffling of steps across the wood flooring. "What brings you out here, Mister Shaw," Jace heard the deputy say. He jerked himself erect and peered through the gloom into the better lit area of the office.

"I'm here to see the prisoner," Shaw said gruffly and reaching for the key ring lying on the desk top. "Alone!" He stated. "Go for a walk. Come back in an hour."

"I...I don't think I'm supposed to do that Mister Shaw," the deputy started to protest. "I know you used to be Sheriff and all, but I don't know if Will's gonna like it."

"Will's not going to know anything about it," Shaw said.

"But...but.. What if he finds out about it?"

"Then he can deal with me. You've got nothing to worry about. Now get out of here!.." His voice went from gruff irritation to commanding authority and he shuffled unsteadily toward the cell. He was just turning the key when he heard the deputy closing the office door behind him.

The cell door swung open wide and the old man stepped through. What little light was left, glinted off the corner of one lens of his spectacles.

THE DEVIL'S JUSTICE

He glared down at Carlin, who was now sitting up on the bunk. He said nothing. His face was gray and placid.

"What do you want?" Carlin growled with bitterness.

The old man remained silent for a moment. Then he said flatly, "I'm letting you go."

"Letting me go?" Carlin almost laughed. "You're not a sheriff anymore. You can't let me go."

"Get up and get out!" The old man ordered.

"Just like that?" Jace said. "Then what? Somebody shoots me escaping? Oh, no. I think I'll just sit tight."

"There's a horse out back. You go out the back door, get on it, ride out and don't come back. No one's gonna be waiting to shoot you down."

"I'm supposed to believe that?"

"If you don't, you'll wind up dancing at the end of a rope. Doesn't seem to me you have much chance but to believe me."

"Why should you help me?"

"I don't want to," the old man said. "It's Jenna I'm helping. God knows she doesn't deserve it, but she's the only daughter I have left."

"She had someone kill Duncan," Jace said. He said it as verification that the old man knew that to be true.

"Yes," Shaw said. "That's why I can't let you hang for something you didn't do."

"You've got to tell Will Parmalee," Jace said.

The old man shook his head. "That wouldn't do any good."

THE DEVIL'S JUSTICE

"Why not?"

"Just get out of here," the old lawman said despondently. "Get as far away from all of this, that you can, and don't come back."

Jace had been pushing the black dun that Russ Shaw had left him, hard for at least a half hour. Remembering how he had mistreated another horse, he slowed the dun to a walk, letting him cool down a bit before bringing him to a halt and dismounted. He loosened the the saddle cinch and let the animal blow. He pulled some tuffs of grass and rubbed the dun down briskly. Once the horse was breathing easily, Carlin took the reins and led the horse on into the darkness.

Russ Shaw had been true to his word. He had not set up any ambush to shoot Jace down while escaping. Carlin had ridden away uneventfully and hopefully unseen. At least he had not detected any followers on his back trail. The moon was full and he could see quite well for this time of night.

While Shaw had been straight with him, Jace had not reciprocated. He had not ridden away from Contention Springs to never return, but had, instead, headed for the Rafter H. There was no way he could leave without clearing his name and Jenna Holt was the only one who could do that. He had to try one more time to get the truth out of her.

He was still walking the black horse when he neared the top of the ridge above the Rafter H ranch house. He picketed the horse just below the skyline and crept forward in the grass until he could look down on the ranch buildings below.

All was still down there, save for a few horses moving about the larger corral behind the barn. Other than that, there was no movement. The bunkhouse was in complete darkness and there didn't seem to be any guards about. The ranch house was dark also except for a light in an upstairs window.

Keeping low and to the shadows, Carlin backed away from the ridge, circled to the west and descended the bank to the flat land below. He approached the ranch house from the rear and crept to a first floor window. He tried it. It was locked. He moved to the left and found another window. This too was locked. He crept around the corner of the house and tried a side window. He was in luck. It moved within the sash as he pushed up on the lower pane. It creaked upward and he slowed his movements, trying not to let the window sound louder. The window was half way up, when Carlin froze in place. A chill of fear swept over him as he felt the hard steel of a gun barrel press deep into the back of his neck. "Hold it right there, cowboy." He recognized the voice of Red Lacy. "Now back away slowly and head for the front door. You want to get inside? You might as well use the door."

Jace refrained from saying anything. He did as he was told and moved toward the front of the house. Lacy kept close behind him and never let up on the pressure of the pistol against his captive's neck.

THE DEVIL'S JUSTICE

When they reached the front door, Jace realized that Riley was also with Lacy. While lacy continued to hold the gun, Riley stepped around them and pounded on the the door. "Mrs. Holt!" He shouted while continuing to bang the wooden panel. "Open up! It's important!"

After a few moments of continual knocking the door latch clicked from inside and the door swung open just enough to see Jenna Holt standing there in nightgown and robe. She held a lighted kerosene lamp in her left hand. "What is it?" She asked, but didn't have to be told when lacy shoved Carlin forward in front of the opening for her to see. He eyes widened with surprise and she stepped back letting the door swing wider open.

"Seems you've got a visitor," Lacy said as he shoved Carlin inside and pushed him to the floor. Jace fell flat on his stomach and rolled over pushing himself to a half sitting position. Riley stepped forward and kicked at him; his boot clipping Carlin just under the chin and driving him backward and crashing into a small table. It fell over and the legs broke as Jace fell into it. He lay in the rubble on his back. Stunned. His jaw throbbing with searing pain and his head clouding with wisps of darkness.

Jenna came forward, still carrying the lamp. "That's enough of that, Riley. Let him be. Jace groaned and rolled over on his side. Broken pieces of the table slid out from under him.

"Get him on his feet!" A deep voice commanded from across the room.

Jace felt himself being pulled to his feet. He was too hurt to struggle as Riley and Lacy stood him him up and held him on rubbery legs that couldn't seem to find the floor. Carlin's head lolled against his chest and he tried to raise it. God, it hurt! The best he could do was to roll his eyes upward in their sockets. As the haze began to clear and his vision returned. At first, there was nothing but a blur before him, but as his eyes strained to focus, he saw. the man standing on the stairway steps, looking down at him. But was it a man? Or was it a ghost? Or was it just his imagination? Or a bad memory?

He jerked his head off his chest, ignoring the pain. The vision was clear now and Carlin's face twisted into a mask of confusion.

"Surprised to see me, Carlin?" The man said and continued descending the steps. He was tucking in his shirttails and his shirt was open at the top revealing the top of his long johns. "When you shoot a man, make sure he's dead, before you leave him behind to die in the snow."

"Drago!" Carlin muttered in disbelief.

"Yes, Al Drago," the man answered stepping down off the bottom step and standing before Jace. He was buttoning his shirt with his left hand. His right hand hung limp at his side. A large scar covered the inside and outside of his hand where Carlin's bullet had passed through, that day on the snow covered mountain.

Jace glanced from Drago to Jenna. "I suppose it's been you and Drago all along."

There was a smug half smile on her face. "You're so dumb, Jace." She chided. "It took you this long to figure it all out." Then she added. "But then again, you were always stupid. You were stupid enough to pass me over for Alice. Sweet, nice Alice," she said. "It was always Alice this and Alice that. Everyone wanted Alice. No one wanted me. Not even Drago, but we needed each other. Two of a kind, you might say."

Drago smiled.

"There was Duncan," Jace said.

"Duncan?" She scoffed. "He wanted Alice too. He always hated you for that, Jace. When Alice married you, Duncan only took me as a consolation prize." She turned and walked to the dining room table and put the lamp down.

She turned and walked back to face Carlin. "I hated all of you," she said bitterly. "I got even with Alice and now I've gotten even with Duncan."

Jace could hardly believe what he was hearing. "You sent Drago and his pals out to burn me out." He had to put it into words. He had to hear himself say it.

"And I suppose, you had Drago kill Duncan too?"

Drago chuckled. "Now how could I do that?" He half lifted his worthless hand.

"I can't use a rifle anymore."

"Then who did? Your goons here?" He tried to twist toward his captors, but Lacy and Riley held him tight.

Drago shook his head from side to side and laughed. "You'd be surprised," he said.

An uncomfortable suspicion began to grow inside Carlin's brain. No! It couldn't be, he thought to himself. Then as if asking for verification, Jace said, "I suppose none of you killed Randy Poole either?"

"Give the man a big cigar," Drago chided. "Maybe he's not so stupid after all," he said to Jenna.

"That's just too bad," Jenna said. "I guess we'll just have to kill him." She turned to Jace. "I'm sorry, Jace. We could have had a good life together."

"You're sick, Jenna," Jace said sorrowfully.

Jenna's eyes blazed with anger, "I said, kill him Drago or I will."

"Sure, sure, Jenna," Drago said. He smiled devilishly. "But first I want to have a little fun with him. I want him him to know the pain I felt when he shot me." He moved closer to Carlin, reached behind him and with his left hand, he plucked Riley's pistol from its holster.

"I want you boys to hold his arm out straight. I'm gonna put a bullet through his hand, just like he did me."

Jace's eyes bulged with fear and he struggled within the confines of the two men holding him. Riley was pulling at his arm and Carlin fought desperately to hold it close to his body. But it was too no avail. The pressure against his elbow sent shards of pain up and down his arm. Slowly he gave in and as Riley pulled his arm almost straight out, Al Drago put the muzzle of the weapon against Carlin's open palm and squeezed the trigger. The pistol roared within the confines of the house and burnt powder billowed up in a cloud of smoke. The bullet ripped through the tissues of Jace's palm and broke the small bones in the back of his hand as the projectile passed through and buried itself in the wall next to the door.

At first Carlin felt no pain, then it settled in. Burning excruciating pain. His insides twisted with nausea and waves of shock flashed in his brain. His knees bent and his captors let him fall to the floor. He writhed violently back and forth, groaning and screaming in pain until he rolled against the leg of the dining room table.

Al Drago stepped forward, smiling and laughing. A loud, gleeful, evil laugh. He pointed the gun directly at Carlin's face and eared back the the hammer.

Through clouded eyes, Jace watched Drago come closer. The corner of the dining room table's table cloth hung just above Carlin's head. Just as Drago pulled the trigger, Carlin reached up with his left hand, clutching the corner of the table cloth and whipping it off. The kerosene lamp flew off the table and struck Drago in the chest. The globe broke, fuel spilled out and caught fire in Drago's shirt as he fell backward, letting his pistol fall to the floor.

Carlin rolled forward, scooping up the sixgun with his remaining good hand, and swinging it toward Red Llacy, who had reacted to the the suddeness, with pistol drawn and brought to bear on Carlin.   Carlin fired first and caught Lacy square in the chest. He fell backward against the wall and slid to the floor dead.

Riley who had relinquished his gun to Drago, had turned and had run for the door. Jace

THE DEVIL'S JUSTICE

swung his pistol and fired. Riley fell face forward out the door he had already opened.

Jenna was screaming wildly as she ran to grasp Drago who was rolling and screaming on the floor with flames engulfing him. Her arms were around him and her robe had caught fire.

The kerosene had spread across the floor by now and and a wall of flame shot up between where Jace lay and where Jenna and Drago struggled. He pushed himself to his feet and tried to make his way through the flames, but they drove him back. The flames were every where now and there was no way to get through.

The screams on the other side subsided and became lost in the sound of the beating flames.

Chapter Ten

The morning sun glinted off the grassy dew. A slight haze was building up from the warming sun predicting another hot day.

Will Parmalee walked lazily around the remains of the Rafter H ranch house. The air was crisp with the smell of charcoal and here and there a few embers still smoldered, even though two days had passed since the fire. He poked among the debris with a stick he had picked up. He didn't know what had caused the fire, but he was sure that Jenna Holt had not survived. He had found remnants of charred bones indicating that she had not perished alone.

He should have felt a pang of remorse, but he didn't. It was just as well that things had turned out this way. Jenna was gone. Jace Carlin was gone. Nobody would ever know the truth now. He smiled to himself.

The smile quickly faded as he turned. His face went grim and he started to settle into a crouch, his arm outstretched to throw the stick away and reach for his gun. He froze, staring at the man before him holding a gun pointed at him. The gun was in the man's left hand. His right hand was bandaged.

"Carlin!" Parmalee exclaimed. "I thought..."

THE DEVIL'S JUSTICE

"You thought I had left town for good," Jace said.

"Russ Shaw said.." He stammered.

"I know. He thought I did what he wanted me to. He should have known me better than that."

"You should have taken his advice, Jace. I still have to take in for Duncan Holt's murder," Will said.

"You know I didn't kill Duncan," Jace said flatly.

Parmalee waited for the rest of it.

"Because you did it yourself, Will."

"Wh..wh.. are you talking about?" Parmalee stammered. "Why would I do such a thing?"

"Because Jenna Holt told you too."

"Wh...why would I do that for her. She meant nothing to me. I'm engaged to Amy Parker. Remember."

"You wouldn't be if you hadn't killed Randy Poole."

"You're crazy," Will protested.

"Somehow, Jenna Holt knew you killed Randy. Then she blackmailed you into killing Duncan and blaming it on me."

"You can't prove that," The Sheriff sneered.

"I don't need to," Carlin said. "We both know it's true. And that's all that matters." He holstered his pistol and let his hand swing loose.

Parmalee tossed away the stick. "Unless you've been practicing with that left hand, you'll never beat me."

"I don't intend to," Jace said. "I'm letting you walk away from here. We're the only ones who know the truth. Go about your business as usual. Tell everyone that Duncan Holt's murderer was Al Drago. That let's me off the hook. I promise Amy Parker will never hear the truth from me."

Will was shaken by the sound of Amy's name. He had done all of this for Amy. He couldn't let her find out now.

"She'd never believe you anyhow," Will said nervously.

"Do you want to take that chance?"

Carlin waited, not really expecting an answer.

Finally, Will Parmalee let out a sigh and straightened, His hand came away from his gun. He stared dully into Jace's placid face for a moment. Then, shook his head and strode past him. He untied his horse, mounted and rode away without looking back.

Jace stood in the roadway for a while, watching the Sheriff disappear into the distance. The sound of horses hoofs approached from behind him. He turned to see Stacy Merritt ride up leading his horse. She halted and gave the reins to him. He swung into the saddle and settled himself.

"You're letting him go? Just like that?" Stacy said.

"Yep. Just like that," Jace said with a smile.

"You sure are a strange one, Jace Carlin. After all your rantings about justice."

"Justice is not mine to reap," He said. "I know that now. Fate has its own way of dealing out Justice. Jenna and Duncan Holt received their share and not by me. Will Parmalee will pay the rest of his life for what he has done."

"What about Amy Parker? Doesn't she deserve better? Shouldn't she know about Will?"

"I don't know," Jace said. "Whatever choices she makes, she'll have to live with. I guess we'll all have to face justice eventually."

"You know what, Carlin?" Stacy Chided. "I do believe you're becoming a philosopher."

" I wouldn't say that exactly," he said. "But now that I can't use this gun hand anymore, I guess I just have to settle down and be a rancher once again."

"It was nice of Russ Shaw to sign your land back over to you now that he's heir to Jenna's estate.

Jace smiled. "Yes, it was. I'm never going to let anyone take it away from me again."

"I don't know about that, cowboy," Stacy giggled. "I just might try to take it myself."

"You're welcome to try." He grinned broadly. They gigged their horses into a trot and rode off.

THE DEVIL'S JUSTICE

THE DEVIL'S JUSTICE

THE DEVIL'S JUSTICE

THE DEVIL'S JUSTICE

www.ingramcontent.com/pod-product-compliance
Lightning Source LLC
Chambersburg PA
CBHW051832170626
46807CB00003B/1148